Emmanuelle Arsan is
young Eurasian – Mary
member of the French
previously served at a
frank, liberated view
brought her internatio
a controversial figure on
Distinguished critic Françoise Giroud of *L'Express*
wrote of her that she 'preaches the "erotic revolution" as seriously as others preach in today's China the "cultural revolution".' The bestselling *Emmanuelle* novels have been turned into films that have broken box-office records all over the world and set new standards for the erotic cinema.

Also by Emmanuelle Arsan

Emmanuelle
Emmanuelle 2
Laure
Nea   A Young Emmanuelle

Emmanuelle Arsan

The Secrets of Emmanuelle

Translated from the French by Celeste Piano

MAYFLOWER
GRANADA PUBLISHING
London Toronto Sydney New York

Published by Granada Publishing Limited
in Mayflower Books 1980

ISBN 0 583 13121 2

A Mayflower UK Original

Granada Publishing Limited
Frogmore, St Albans, Herts AL2 2NF
and
3 Upper James Street, London W1R 4BP
866 United Nations Plaza, New York, NY 10017, USA
117 York Street, Sydney, NSW 2000, Australia
100 Skyway Avenue, Rexdale, Ontario, M9W 3A6, Canada
PO Box 84165, Greenside, 2034 Johannesburg, South Africa
CML Centre, Queen & Wyndham, Auckland 1, New Zealand

Set, printed and bound in Great Britain by
Cox & Wyman Ltd, Reading
Set in Intertype Times

Contents

I. Eve and After

I loved no matter how – and did not love.

Nitya Phenkun: *My siren sister*

Pussy Power

As a child I believed that boys were unable to make love. They were incapable of so doing because they had no appropriate organ.

Love, in my view, was only to be made with the pussy. (I was living in England, and like everyone in my circle used this word to denote the gash – as yet hairless – of my sex, and of course those of other girls. From a very early age this particular little cat interested me far more and afforded me infinitely greater pleasure than the real kittens people gave me as presents.) Thus only females, whether adults or not, were able to make love. I already had the feeling that Nature was unjust, and was discovering that the dice are loaded from birth; but more than anything I was really glad to have been born with such an advantage!

I very soon realized that this privilege brought with it an obvious responsibility: I had to treat boys well in order to make them forget their shame and console their inevitable grief at being so deprived.

Where did I get such ideas from? Quite frankly, I don't know. But I do understand all too well how useful they've been to me throughout my life and the debt of gratitude I owe them.

I was conceived far from here, on the sand and the salt, amid the sexual odour of freshly caught fish. My mother was barely fifteen. She had gone with a relative to revisit her old village of red wood and stilts on the shores of a sea gaudy with coral, white with jellyfish and black with sharks. My prospective father met her by pure chance on this beach, under this sun. At that time he too was very young: he was studying by himself to become a town-dweller and a traveller. They made love without even really bothering to get acquainted.

I was born before they really got to know each other. In the meanwhile my mother had known other men and my father other women. Because of me, perhaps, they married and then never again left one another.

I have never seen for myself the village I describe. My parents did not return. When I left my native land with them I was just a baby, too young to remember or think of returning.

I grew up in Europe, then moved about so often that now I feel at home anywhere. I don't have the sense of belonging to one nation rather than another, nor to one race, nor to one clearly defined – or limited – culture. None the less, I don't think of myself as stateless; there is a freedom in being a stranger which counts for more than any likeness.

It is not, then, surprising that my recollections of childhood, when I evoke them, are bewildering and disturbing. So many adults have forgotten their formative years that they no longer recognize themselves in the real children they meet or hear about. They forget that at four or five they too were all sex, only interested in pleasure, capable of any and every impudence. No doubt I am unique, among all these voluntary amnesiacs, in remembering how things really were.

When I was six, my sister was four; this age difference in no way prevented our sharing the same tastes and desires. And I very clearly recall that the desire which most obsessed us was to see female sexes – *pussies*.

We had many occasions to satisfy this urge. To begin with, naturally, we would spend much time each day perfecting the mutual contemplation and simultaneous manipulation of our own little pussies. And we admired our mother's very much. We wouldn't for the world have missed her arrival in the bathroom. We would rush to lean over the edge of the bath and look into the clear water. Even more than her face, which would be smiling tenderly at our curiosity and zeal, it was her pubis, her vagina and breasts that seemed to us to merit the most adoring devotion and prolonged scrutiny.

Yet other women also interested us. The most memorable at that time was an English red-head who came to stay with us for several months and whom we immediately deemed 'almost as beautiful' as our mother and 'almost as young'. In fact she was some five years her junior, being only about sixteen or seventeen herself. At first she was worried lest we burst into her room unexpectedly, with the avowed intention of seeing her in bed. Our interest in her had been aroused the moment we discovered she didn't sleep in the nude. Though our parents and we ourselves did, we also knew that many people swathed themselves in nightdresses and pyjamas, and we thought this was silly.

This Mildred soon changed her ways, however, and we asked her in all sincerity and seriousness if she would let us see her pussy. She seemed temporarily disconcerted, thought about it for a moment, then, quite decided, threw off her sheets and told us: 'There, look!' The novelty and luxuriance of the russet tuft dazzled us . . .

It only took a few days after that for Mildred to become more intimate still. She certainly would not have dared make the first moves herself, but we had embraced and kissed her so thoroughly and often that she'd have had to have been made of stone to resist these advances.

Yet until that moment my sister and I had not the least theoretical or practical idea about physical love, although we thought we did. We simply made a fetish of the female body and we were discovering for ourselves, with the capacity for invention common to all young children, the gestures required for expressing sensuous admiration and desire.

Much later, when an artist uncle arrived in London, one who preferred nudes to apples, we never gave him any peace until he let us hang about his studio endlessly. Neither he nor his models (he had the good taste and the knack of choosing beautiful ones) seemed to think that we could look at a naked woman other than 'innocently'. He and they soon realized, however, that these staring sessions got us into a highly excited state. We weren't at all embarrassed by masturbating in front of them to our hearts' content and passing detailed remarks at considerable length upon the charms of the young woman at whom we were gazing. In order to amuse her, for we understood that her work was boring, we would invent unlikely erotic adventures into the bargain, and these we would generously attribute to her, invariably petrifying her in every case. Let us hope that the ideas we put into her head were to our uncle's advantage!

The strange thing is, though, that these stories, like all those we dreamed up, spoken or unspoken, were always exclusively homosexual, as well they might be. Had we not decided once and for all that boys could not be anyone's partners in love, not even of their own sex? Sexuality, in our eyes, was thus not just homosexual, but more specifically and uniquely lesbian. Needless to say we were completely unaware of such terminology and our discussions rejected all categories so as to stick closely to the facts!

We recognized boys for what they were, i.e. sexless creatures, unerotic and forever barred from any inclination to pleasure. But that did not delight us or make us want to laugh or mock: quite the opposite – we felt sorry for boys. We really pitied them with all our hearts, and had we known how to express this (we did later!) it would have been with our bodies too.

Not only did their lot seem wretched to us, since they lacked that pussy which gave us females so much beauty and pleasure but, far worse, their little bit of flesh wasn't even fun to piss with!

Pissing, as a matter of fact, had only a symbolic significance for us. It was not just a sign of intimacy by which we set great store among ourselves (to piss with another girl was already to love her); but more importantly, the entrance of the urethra (at an age when the clitoris was more of a promise than a reality) was the undoubted focus of our pleasurable sensations, and thus of our solitary or mutual caresses, of lick and tickle.

Since this little orifice gave us satisfaction, how could we understand that a boy with his different equipment might derive the same pleasure? We were convinced that pissing would hurt him.

As far as we were concerned everything about the way boys were made and their behaviour made us pity them. It was quite futile for them to try to prove us wrong: such desperate attempts only served to convince us all the more of their misfortune. This they were trying hard to hide because they were ashamed of it – and shame to us was the ugliest feeling we knew – and the most alien.

Our main illusion was definitely in believing that women never felt shame. On the other hand we felt touching and unlimited compassion whenever one of our male friends would toil at shaking and rubbing his hapless sprig of a penis to make it (with a success to which we were strangely insensitive) swell and grow hard. We would think of the pain it must be causing him! And to what purpose? The poor lad must have had a really warped sense of pride to inflict pain upon himself voluntarily just to make us believe in a satisfaction which we knew to be a sham.

His real aim, as we well guessed, was to impress us: we were kind-hearted enough not to add to his problems by letting him know how bad this impression was!

Long afterwards, when we were better informed about boys' sexuality my sister and I would laugh at those Freudian theories of 'penis-envy'. I certainly don't deny that many women do go through this psychological phase, but I feel justified in doubting whether the process is universal. My sister and I are living proof that there are exceptions to all rules, even those of the Viennese genius.

Today it seems to me worth reflecting a while on this good fortune. Indeed, I wouldn't consider my childhood experiences worth recounting had they not helped me (and perhaps others too) to understand one other peculiarity. This one played so dominant a role in my life that today I am almost tempted to look on it as the only one of my experiences which really counts – for me and for everyone.

I have never been scared of boys. Consequently, I've never scared *them* either.

At first sight this absence of intimidation might seem trivial. It isn't. More widespread than any other impulse, more tyrannical even than the libido, fear dominates the relationships of human beings. Every animal fears another, men fear other men; and above all, men are afraid of women and women of men.

Do all women really scare all men? Yes! This is another truth which must be recognized by both sides: men are scared of women, even more than women are scared of men.

Doubtless because the latter are vainer than the

former, or because women are craftier and more devious, the opposite has been held to be true. A truth which, when one examines it more closely, seems riddled with contradictions, since one is more afraid of the unknown than the known. The woman who has given birth to man surely knows him better than he does himself.

A subconscious fear can do more harm than a conscious one. The fact that men and women terrorize one another without admitting as much is at the root of their great misfortunes. For as long as neither sex agrees to face these fears, to analyse and judge them honestly, for as long as neither will try to seek their causes the battle of the sexes will continue.

I myself have never waged war on men any more than I have on women. I feel a bond with each. I find it possible and desirable to be allied to both. I probably succeeded in this because I've never been afraid of them and because when very young I loved them equally. I loved women, by wanting to see and touch their bodies and wanting them to touch me; I loved men by understanding their pain, knowing them to be private, deprived, helpless, forsaken, solitary, fearful, incomplete, ashamed and unhappy despite all their swaggering. Thus I sought as best I could to make men and women happy so that life might be less cruel for everyone, myself included.

I'm sure my little girl's naïvety will make plenty of older people smile. Yet so many years later I still believe this innocence sprang from a fortunate intuition to which I owe much of my happiness and because of which many men and women must have shared that happiness. At the very least, I have been indebted to this intuition and have always regarded it as a piece of good luck.

It must be said though that I have heard a lot about

pussy since those days when I thought of it as a fortunate privilege and a delightful inequality. But since then I have heard it talked about in a way I find frightening.

Certain feminists for instance (initially in the USA then elsewhere), have attracted considerable publicity by trying to popularize the slogan 'Pussy Power'. If it simply meant restoring to our cunts their innate power as well as referring to our behaviour towards men, I would applaud wholeheartedly. This cause is mine.

But in reality this slogan really means 'Women are superior to men!' And if it does, I don't agree with it!

I do not wish to dominate men any more than I want them to dominate me. Nor do I, who have never been overawed by them, want to scare them off. I want them to know and understand me and hope that some of them will end up loving me. I want those I desire to desire me; want those who make me come to come themselves; want those I teach to instruct me in turn; want those I liberate to free me; want those I help become men to encourage me to be a woman, and for those whom I want to see happy to believe in the possibility of their happiness and mine.

Yet how shall I realize this all-consuming project if men are afraid of me? How are we to live in harmony on the same planet if they fear my power, believe in my deadly and fatal superiority, bow to my authority, bow to my merest whims and cynically angle for my favours?

As long as we tremble whenever we stand face to face, how shall we ever discover if it's possible for us to face the world together?

All things considered, have we anything else or better to do on this Earth than try to know ourselves?

Thus I will always prefer 'pussy knowledge' to 'pussy power', since the former advocates unity between the sexes instead of division. Nevertheless, this knowledge can never be other than loving. So one might as well say that everything still remains to be done before men and women are united.

Though I was young when I embarked upon it, my amatory exploration still left me lamentably ignorant.

And probably I didn't delight as many boys as I should have done or didn't do so in the right way.

Be that as it may, one thing is sure: myth needs mystery. Knowledge happily buries myths and fears. And the history of our species, like it or not, is reduced to those concealed phobias from which the progress of knowledge has delivered us.

No doubt we are completely wrong to think that any good can come of secrecy. Perhaps we are even right to fear it. Otherwise, if what is hidden is not harmful why go on concealing it?

So we women must not wait for others to set an example: let us proclaim the end of the game of hide-and-seek! Let us truly make a gesture of solidarity which will serve as a test: if we are truly neither afraid nor ashamed of our pussies, let us solemnly and publicly stop concealing them.

If men cannot bear the sight, then we'll know for certain the difference between honesty and hypocrisy. We'll know the trail-blazers from the cowards.

Our freedom and courage have been faked long enough. If we don't want our power to remain simply make-believe let us show at last – for ourselves as much as others – our bodies for real.

As a little girl then, I was not afraid of boys. So that even today men are not afraid of me.

But I am almost alone in not getting them into a blind panic! For in reality all men are scared of women.

Here of course we're clearly far from the well-worn routes which the feminists prefer to tread. Nowadays more than ever fashion, and therefore propriety, welcomes discussion (in books and newspapers) and demonstration (in films and on TV) only of the physical and mental brutalities which men perpetrate upon women.

For some time the latest fashion for militant feminists (who are not above borrowing the most chauvinist methods) has been to daub the slogan: 'No more rape!' all over Paris.

OK, so they are sick and tired of being violated, but at the risk of sticking my neck out, I'd like to ask these protesters a serious question – have they taken the trouble to wonder why certain men rape certain women? Is it because the women fear the men or vice versa?

Men rape out of revenge. And why are they taking revenge? Rapists are rarely recruited from the ranks of those male chauvinists who reduce women to a subservient role, and confine them to the kitchen, the washing-up, the laundry and care of babies, or who exploit their labour in offices and factories. On the whole rapists are weak, timid, and humiliated people exasperated by their lack of success with women, whom they don't understand. They cannot bear the contradictory myths about women which they themselves have made: they imagine them to be cockteasers, nymphos, whores, unapproachable, frigid. They try to exorcize through a ritual violence the overwhelming panic they experience whenever they think of these imagined amazons with *their* potential violence and of the impossibility of ever pleasing them. Through the denial of others they exorcize their solitary obsessions and sense of rejection. They respond with actual physical terror to the invisible psychic terror which the unreasonable, illogical strength of women (whom they consider irrational and beyond logic) brings to bear against them.

This is why it is true that many men become, in their own ways, potential rapists. Those of them who do not sexually abuse women beat them up and degrade them when they get the chance, each in his own style – emotionally, intellectually, culturally, professionally, or socially – because they want to reduce women to a state of helplessness, through their need for security. They want to break them in so as not to be broken by them. It proves they think women formidable and this drives them wild.

I recently read Jomo Kenyatta's book *Facing Mount Kenya.* Before he became a revolutionary leader and then Kenyan head of state, the future *Mzee* was an ethnologist. In this capacity he had studied his tribe, the Kikuyu, discovering one curiously instructive legend.

In the dawn of time, so the Kikuyu say, women ruled absolutely over men. They were all-powerful, tyrannical and cruel. Stronger, more resourceful and better organized than the men, they would compel their males to perform the hardest and meanest tasks. They deprived them of food, pleasure and freedom and would not allow them any participation at all in tribal or domestic matters. The women scornfully dominated their sex lives, their family life and their social status. From cradle to grave they treated men like second-class citizens, sickly children or mentally retarded beings. They would not permit them to have personal aspirations or, collectively, to initiate any change. The women compelled them for all time to behave according to the image the former had moulded for them, and the women would not even speculate that 'the lower nature' of these congenitally handicapped beings could ever qualify them for the dignified jobs and creative functions of society. They saw that men were born different from themselves and because of this judged them 'inferior' and innately destined for domesticity.

This *pussy power* – among the most radical and strict our species has ever known – made the masculine half of humanity appallingly unhappy. Yet the women refused to understand and remedy their suffering. They considered that the world was created thus and the status quo should be respected.

The 'pussycrats' of prehistoric Kenya did not wish their men harm: on the contrary, they loved them deeply. They had no doubt that female supremacy existed by virtue of natural law (or divine right, as their High Priestess might well have explained it) and operated quite as much 'for the good of' those interesting, flawed and fragile creatures called men as to the advantage of their protectresses. The complaints and demands of the oppressed would change neither their rulers' convictions nor the system.

The male Kikuyu, after centuries of degradation and resignation, finally had enough of the system. After their more open attempts at rebellion had been easily put down one after the other by the omnipotent female ruling class, in desperation the men resorted to trickery and secret, concerted action.

After a number of fruitless attempts, they succeeded in getting all the women pregnant at the same time.

When the women were almost in labour and so found themselves – momentarily yet simultaneously – in a relatively weak position, the conspirators seized military, political and economic power, and never again let go of it.

Naturally they took a merciless and thoroughgoing revenge upon the vanquished for their past excesses.[1] In this way the present relationship between the sexes came about.

This story may seem naïve to most of us. Wrongly so, for if its historical authenticity is doubtful, its value as psychological document is practically universal: it describes not merely the superstitions of a so-called savage race but also, in a crude form, the behaviour of all modern civilization.

The sexual order to which we are witness is one of *reprisals*. It expresses the primitive reactions of combatants who have emerged the precarious victors of a long war and who, like all conquerors, live in fear of a reversal of fortunes and the revenge of the vanquished. Men treat women badly not because they think them powerless and know them to be at their mercy, but because they deem them capable of once again locating an ancestral strength temporarily lost, and because they have retained the horrible memory of a time when they themselves had to submit to that strength.

[1] *Author's Note:* The atrocious custom of clitoridectomy still practised in Kenya (and elsewhere! See p. 97 *A World without Clitoris*) in all probability dates back to this episode, or more specifically to the origin of this myth, although Jomo Kenyatta tries awkwardly to find 'hygienic' reasons for it and to justify it as 'female circumcision'. Actually by cutting off the clitoris at puberty men not only prevent women from attaining climax, they ritually take back from them a phallic symbol of power. To them a woman who has become purely vaginal no longer seems capable of ruling over them. And the thing is, they're probably right! For a woman the means of testing her freedom and strength is by way of conscious clitoral auto-eroticism. When she experiences the feeling of self-confidence and achievement accompanying the orgasm

Such a vision certainly contradicts the image Freud has bequeathed us of *the primal horde*. Yet the founder of psychoanalysis himself could not, any more than the Kikuyu or I, explain away the irrefutable material evidence of the organization of primitive societies. He too used to base his theories on residual psychological observations. No matter how good these were, he could not see the present in its totality nor imagine the past. In particular, having chosen to examine the individual more attentively than the mass, he sometimes neglected to take into account the latter's role in the formation of character, ideas and actions. In fact – and we know this today more clearly than he did – what endows some with mental and social strength and confines others to a continuing state of weakness is not so much their innate inclinations and sex-drives as the world into which they were born.

A society whose resources are at men's disposal from birth ensures male supremacy, just as a capitalist regime offers opportunities only to rich children. An alternative civilization, in which woman had priority, would lead to male submission to women.

Now the fascinating paradox of the present system as we see it is this: the subconscious minds of men function everywhere as if retaining the buried memory of an unbearable domination women had exercised over and *against* them!

When? They cannot say: not everyone has the memory of a Kikuyu![2] Yet this tradition obscurely im-

---

she has reached through knowing how to make use of her clitoris (alone and effectively – i.e. without needing penis or penetration) she is doing something quite other than discovering a 'narcissism' which is all too often a figment of masculine analysts' imaginations: she is learning about the mental and physical autonomy of pleasure – and of the individual.

[2]*Author's Note:* I quite expect even the most tolerant of my women

printed upon their genes still disturbs them to the point of blinding them to present-day actualities: they go on treating like deposed tyrants those who no longer have the power to enslave them.

But is it really so certain that they no longer have such power? Do women really live only to serve men and to turn themselves into forced collaborators in their ambitions and pleasures?

The error which has been made, and is still being made today, of a one-sided evaluation of the conjugal and domestic balance of power probably goes on perpetuating the misunderstanding and war between the sexes. No peace or collaboration is possible between former enemies if neither makes a move towards sincerity and loyalty.

And the first piece of plain speaking consists of recognizing that women, in their own general explanation of their lot, quite glibly demonstrate their utter dishonesty.

Their subordination is sometimes real, but all too

---

readers to end up showing some impatience on seeing me return, apparently smugly, to this 'legend'. Don't I understand, I hear them say, that the selfish and cynical African males invented it simply to justify by hindsight the indignities – clitoridectomy being only one example – to which they still submit their wives and daughters? By pretending they want to guard against the recurrence of a feminine despotism that probably never historically existed, their natural (and amply documented) sadism casts them in the leading roles.

All very well, but there may also be speculation as to why they feel this bewildering need to saddle themselves with a humiliating past. Isn't it evidence of an inferiority complex which reverts compulsively to a traumatic experience of their collective – or individual – prehistory? What then can that experience be? It is hardly difficult to give this basic fear its real name, which is unfortunately not confined to the Kikuyu! All men are marked by it for life: we shall return to this later.

Need I add that this explanation is a justification neither of men's brutality nor of the stupidity of women who sometimes allow clitoridectomy 'out of love' – or what they *think* is love. (cf. Maureen's story in the second part of this book).

often they themselves have wanted it. They have asked their men to take care of them, to look after them, to think of and attend to their welfare. If they have lost some of their freedom, it is because freedom seemed to them less desirable than comfort and security.

Does a woman usually get married in order to be free – or to be assured of a future that conforms with the values and conventions of her background? Can she expect to be treated as an equal by a husband when she wants from the very start to be kept, protected and possessed by him?

But there's worse to come. Knowingly or not, too many women marry to take on the mantle of that very mother who (to their husbands) was the incarnation of strength and inspired them with their first fear of authority.

Ought the wife to be surprised, consequently, if the man reacts towards her with embarrassment, fear, and a secret desire for revenge which maternal domination unwittingly creates within all her sons?

The ancestral female power I described earlier, towards which men still bear incredible rancour and of which they remain in awe, has probably never ruled kingdoms. On the other hand it still reigns in every household, within every mind and heart. We fear what creates us. We have tried inventing gods so that this power can be distanced from us, may stem from other flesh than the mother's. Yet we no longer believe in progenitor-gods and our mother's womb remains horribly close.

But the child cannot equal its creator. As long as men regard themselves as the creations of woman they will fear her and dream of no longer believing in her, just as they have (almost) succeeded in no longer believing in God.

If women really wish for that happy day when they

can share with men the same Earth, they must first work to purge men of the after-effects of their faith. They must teach them that woman is not a goddess. She does not want to be feared or enslaved, she just wants to be known and loved.

If she cannot manage to substitute human desires for mythological relationships, woman will stay forever incomprehensible to man. Man will go on hating woman as much as he secretly hates God.

Above all, he will know how to continue dominating her. Because man only survives through bringing the power of his intellect to bear upon what makes him afraid.

The Anti-Eve, the Future Eve and the love of the stars

My feminist readers, quick to take offence and well-versed in polemic, are doubtless wondering whether Emmanuelle Arsan has accepted some kind of bribe in return for launching a campaign to denigrate women. One, furthermore, which will reassure and strengthen male attitudes of superiority and condescension.

But what makes *feminists* so militant?

If it's equality of the sexes they want to establish, they should become biologists not agitators or legislators: perhaps then they might be able to produce new species of humans from their test-tubes, undifferentiated by penis and vagina, breasts and moustaches, chromosomes and hormones. For as long as such causes of inequality endure, to talk as if morality and law could ignore them is just hot air.

If the true aim of feminism is a society in which one sex will be freed from the other's power, then I am for that too! But on one condition, that such liberation is mutual. For you must be honest enough to recognize that sexual domination is not the prerogative of one sex.

Women will not help make life happier and fairer by claiming with clear consciences to be totally blameless. To a great extent they are themselves responsible for ills suffered at the hands of men. So they will only succeed in changing male attitudes if they themselves first decide to change many of their own views as wives and the way they behave as mothers.

They can do it. Change is easier for women than men because a *cultural* inheritance affords more scope for transformation than a *natural* inheritance. And the fear women have of men is an essentially cultural phenomenon, a tradition they have been taught, while men's fear of women is natural and instinctive.

It is unnatural for a woman to fear a being whom she has carried for nine months inside herself then suckled, nursed and swaddled; whom she has taught to eat, talk, laugh and walk – a being she has created. When this being is fully grown she cannot in all sincerity believe in her avowed fear of him. This fear is mostly sham, affectation; a selfish attitude; a fear born of calculation.

Often it is convenient to let oneself be thought weak or weaker than one really is: this can be a winning ploy. Women play at being in distress because their ultimate ambition is to win. The real rules of relationships between the sexes are those of sport, business and war.

These rules obtain in many areas, today as in the past, to women's advantage quite as much as men's. Thus it is, primarily, that women's acknowledged reputation for weakness gives them the option of simple and effective trickery – of tactical evasions which they turn to their advantage with presence of mind, skill, composure and sheer nerve, so as to get what they want from men.

Convention, however, can only be fully satisfied if women take care never to refer to their privileges and on the contrary endlessly complain about their helplessness and misery, always portraying themselves as born losers, even when this is patently untrue.

This consciously defeatist pose not only ensures that their acquired privileges will not be disputed, but also continually increases their chances of gaining more. The chronically guilty conscience with which the woman thus saddles her adversary-partner thus weakens the latter's resistance . . .

Isn't this just the treacherous indictment one might expect from a shameless pornographer whose trade it is to supply her male chauvinist bosses with their regular ration of woman-as-object?

Poor discredited men! I know them better than their attackers – I who make love with them for the same reasons they do so with me: out of pleasure, friendship, tenderness, imagination, hope. I know what they're looking for: as well as a bed-mate they also want an interesting participant in their conversations, an accomplice in their concerns, a loyal ally in their struggles and reverses.

And do they find these dreamed-of companions in the unidentified objects women have always been to them; in the inscrutable faces that scare and startle them; in the elusive bodies of which they are ignorant, and which appear to hail from outer space? Can they trust these alien beings who simultaneously tease them and deny them, tempt them and resent their desires, wound them and yet are the first to bleed, the only ones to weep?

What feelings, finally, do you think these contradictory strangers inspire within them, other than an incomprehension which ends in real dread, an ill-temper that resorts to blows, and an anxiety to protect themselves from women's brilliance, malice and strength?

Yet despite their fears and grudges, men go on admiring women and wanting to love them. Is this because they are particularly stupid? Or do they have a need, more instinctive than cultural, to pit themselves against whatever is different from themselves? Or is it because men cannot help dreaming of other worlds and hoping for infinite marvels from them?

I mention other worlds advisedly. Though, of course, physically absurd if psychologically inevitable, the theory of woman's extra-terrestrial origin has always been part of masculine mythology.

Whether as in the past woman was required to be a mystery, a poetic metaphor, or to become in our more sceptical times a science fiction subject, this tradition has gradually discovered in her archangel or demon, visiting incubus or visited sybil, Atlantean survivor or emigrant from burnt-out planets. This is not to say that all men are equally credulous towards these fables, but sometimes it only takes imagination to jog a buried memory: so many dead women, more fantastic than any living woman, have left their mark upon our race's legendary past that our memories have understandably remained haunted by them!

Did Lilith – the first of these immortal phantoms, Eve's diametric opposite and mythical double – come from real sky or imagined Hell? Was she an actual lover or the perverse wish of primitive mythmaking instincts? Probably no Adam ever knew her, and none of his descendants has given any clear account of her.

And yet, feared and admired, desired and shunned, loved and hated since the Creation, this being of indeterminate gender has left a mark upon man, influencing future sexual relationships more fundamentally than the greedy, silly, unscrupulous and sly Eve whom Jehovah in pettily semantic mood labelled 'Woman, because she was taken out of man'. (Genesis II: 23)[1]

Taken from his body – but what of Lilith? Isn't it appealing to imagine that Adam himself drew her out of his mind? Which might explain how this Anti-Eve, far more ambiguous and perverse, more daring and less successful than God's Eve had been, still managed to retain, in man's eyes, the incomparable merit of being *free* – because she thus deliberately compensated for the original Eve's final surrender to the conservatism, obscurantism and blinkered, hopeless inflexibility of an alien power.

Was Lilith imperfect? Indeed she was. But she was

[1]*Translator's Note:* The Authorized Version in fact ascribes these words to Adam, not Jehovah.

also infinitely perfectible and consequently the most human creation ever dreamed of.

Man, who might easily have remained just one more animal among many, has turned inventor and creative artist by remaking what he creates, tirelessly recasting his work, changing its direction and shape as he renews his self-examination concerning his own desires and actions, never content with himself or others, pushing back the frontiers of his universe, dangerously tinkering with his destiny and continuing – in the teeth of reason and common sense – to believe that the day will come when his dreams are realized.

This obsessive desire for perfection is surely responsible for the crazy ideas about women and exciting images of them which men evolve and which, consequently, make them intolerant of women's reality.

Man can only bear the strangeness of woman by assuming that she needs to recover a perfection which transcends him (who regards himself as down to earth, careworn, limited). This idea he finds annoying, yes, but stimulating too. Imagining what woman *could* be, hence *should* be, and making conjectural comparisons with the women he knows, he concludes that he is under no illusions about them, because they are only rough drafts, accidentally ruined, which mustn't make him pessimistic about the final masterpiece.

Doesn't this masterpiece exist only in a hypothetical future in which man hopes to find instant perfection among other women than the ones he has hitherto known, different women he has not so far been lucky enough to meet? 'Other women', clearly, have always been for every man the only women to embody that ideal perfection of which his own wife deprives him. No matter if one of these others deceives him in her turn: incorrigible optimist, till his dying day he will persist in mythically reinventing woman and transferring to this myth the admiration and love of which he is capable and of which real women show themselves unworthy.

No one understood better than Hadaly – *The Future Eve* of Philippe Villiers de l'Isle Adam's story – the promise man expects of woman, which can never be kept.

Since this Eve was created by man, she knew from the start the creator's temporary esteem for and passionate devotion to his creation. Yet from the moment she became the most beautiful, the most perfect, most completely coherent and best loved of women, she sensed that her inventor would soon look elsewhere, towards some further objective, and that he knew himself quite resourceful enough to reach this destination some day.

I always feel sad to think of this sister with her artificial flesh, who would go out to look up at the sky and 'brood in the night upon the gleam of dead stars'. She guessed, in her brave sorrow, that despite space and time those stars always glimpsed by man, light-years away, would be her rivals for ever.

Just as he draws ever nearer to them, man, who had at first admired and feared these other-worldly enigmas, dreams of them without such apprehension and unease, bestowing upon them a saner desire.

If women want men to treat them with some modicum of that love men reserve for their starrier longings, they too should strip themselves gradually of their mystery. Let them give the lie to their reputation for inaccessibility and stop burning to ashes those who touch them.

When women let men look their fill at them, let men boldly reach out towards them; when women give up shouting 'Rape!' the moment a man tries to explore and know them, they will not be degraded – any more than the stars themselves can be – and perhaps they'll become as interesting.

The only thing which should annoy a star, if it has any sense at all, is that ignorant and fearful people continue to believe it is remote when really it is close at hand.

The dairymaid and the milk drinkers

Men depend on women. They depend on women for physical satisfaction and the preservation of their societies, and also to honour and perpetuate their myths – indeed, for everything really important to them.

Yet they are still so restricted by their attitudes of mind and behaviour that they make ill use of some of their needs so as to disguise others. This is the main function of their mythologies.

However paradoxical it may seem at first sight, the modern myth of motherhood was actually designed to distort woman's original image. In the eyes of today's moralizing male, a mother is a sexless woman who neutralizes the threat of the real woman.

Anyone who knows any homosexuals realizes that however much they delude themselves, many of them still rely on the real woman even more than the mythical mother. They still worship the real, sexual woman even though they avoid her. Many homosexual men reject women only reluctantly, from confusion or fear. And most of those desperately trying to find something better, implicitly or explicitly see heterosexuality as 'normal' and their own desires as deviance.

In the long run their experience is basically no different from almost every man's: before seeming utterly unattractive to him, woman is an ideal, i.e. an unreal desire, a beautiful fantasy.

Such admiration rules, or misleads, them often without their realizing it. At the price of considerable unhappiness they convince themselves that they only feel attracted to their own sex, their heroes or friends. They imagine other men are easier to approach, more compatible intellectually, emotionally and physically, than women. But those who decide permanently to do without women, since women have betrayed that ideal perfection devised for them, are left with sorrowful consciences and ungratifiable desires. The thought of the love they might have had for a real female lover remains with them as a bitter after-taste.

If it were true, as the feminists imagine, that men despise women, they would not make such heavy weather of wanting to forget or replace women, they would simply pay them no heed. Even homosexuals rarely succeed in being *totally* uninterested in the opposite sex.

To understand the nostalgia with which even the most apparently incorrigible of men can endow them, women should read the admirable words addressed directly to them by a philosopher, known and respected the world over, who happens to be unashamedly homosexual. The quotation is from an essay dealing not specifically with women, but in fact almost wholly devoted to the topic and defence of sodomy:

'I would like to lie down beside them, like someone on the point of fainting, like a bride-to-be . . . I would like to draw closer, foolishly, to the bodies from which anguish has always distanced me . . . What will it all matter a month or a year from now? I know it will happen to myself or someone else. I know that a mouth or hand makes a penis or clitoris erect. Need these mouths and hands necessarily be of the same sex as their owners, on the pretext that police everywhere require them to belong to the opposite sex? . . . There are two sexes on this earth, but only one sexual desire.'[1]

[1]*Author's Note:* From 'Arseholes Possessed' in *Three Million Perverts* (*Recherches*, March 1973. Unsigned article, author Michel Foucault).

Those to whom such language might seem too academic would anyhow do well to wonder why so many homosexuals have recourse to the services of prostitutes. Female prostitutes, that is, although there's no lack of male ones! It's worth realizing that even those males drawn towards their own sex[2] continue to feel 'the need for a woman'.

Men have mythologized female sexuality. By means of this myth women control men.

Man, on the other had, *is not mythologized by woman: woman's sexual myth has always been woman herself.*

Traditionally woman's sexual goal is to be a woman for a man, not to ask a man to satisfy *her* desires, *her* fantasies, *her* need for orgasm. In this tradition, making love, for the woman, means being loved. This is, then, just the opposite of renunciation, resignation and submission: to be loved means having power over the lover and being in a position to dominate him.

The day these relationships change and sexual myths become reciprocal, with women openly desiring men in the same way that men desire women; the day women speak out and declare their desire to *men*, looking for men in their erotic quest just as men look for women, with the same intention and as frankly – then a real women's liberation and *men's* too, might become possible. What is more, women might recover the dignity

[2]*Author's Note: Sincerely* drawn. I am not here questioning the validity or specificity of homosexual desire: this much I must be granted, as a woman who also loves women! I do not claim to describe homosexual psychology, but merely focus attention upon one aspect of it which links up with my theme: the myth which man, through fear, has made out of woman. This myth of womanhood is in other respects radically different from those created by lesbian or bisexual women.

which their ancient, secret, shameful domination of men through sex has caused them to lose.

Shameful domination: really? To judge that, let us return to the subject of prostitutes, in their own way the women most skilful at arousing love.

Isn't it miraculous that *these* women are universally indispensable whereas, in comparison, male prostitutes are not. (Proof of this being that the latter work overtime at getting self-publicity. Prosperous capitalists take good care not to sink to such exhibitionism.)

The stock answers to this question all postulate the subjection of women to male chauvinist power. It is hard to imagine a more absurdly superficial explanation! The most cursory reflection is enough to demonstrate that the balance of power in fact works precisely the opposite way. Whoever cannot do without someone is dominated, mentally and physically, by the one satisfying this need. Men who have an emotional need for prostitutes depend on prostitutes. The prostitutes do not depend upon them.

With all due respect to many a rigorous theorist, economic oppression is not the only form of injustice that rules the earth. Man does not live by bread alone! The tyranny of moral myths is quite as maddening and degrading as poverty. And one of their worst aspects is that they are generally endured without any possibility of rebellion against them. They form networks of domination which have been *assimilated*.

But to simplify the argument, even if one sticks to the plain and simple laws of market economy, it must be conceded that these rarely operate to the supplier's loss and the buyer's gain. Of course a dairymaid depends on her clients' money; yet these clients think they need milk even more than she needs money. She could, if pushed, get another job. They don't even consider doing without milk . . .

Besides, the dairymaids show that they know where the real power lies (without worrying overmuch about the pros and cons) by going on strike whenever they think necessary. Have you ever heard of a milk-drinkers' strike?[3]

It is true that the latter too could get worked up and demolish the dairies, for men regularly do meet women's demands with inordinate violence. Yet even when they are better organized and enclose their adversaries behind harem bars (or inside kitchens) they are admitting their fear and acting, in a sense, out of admiration. How can they fail to see that such unreasonable passions not only put their prisoners in the right but also do themselves a disservice in the long run? As every houri or cook (no fools they) knows very well!

But I am under no illusions. The criticism I am making of sexual power politics goes too far against current fashion for me not to be branded, sooner or later, as a reactionary or an Aunt Thomasina.[4]

The meditations of one or another champion of *Pussy Power*, however, come nowhere near convincing me that all-out war against men is the only activity worthy of woman's talents. Proof of this is the pain I felt on reading an article by the most fanatical Italian feminist, Dacia Maraini.[5]

This self-styled Marxist apparently suffers from an inexplicable incapacity to transcend the most banal superficialities of sexual relationships. She is irritated to

[3]*Author's Note:* Even boycotting coffee does not make much impression, where coffee has become an absolute necessity.

[4]Compare the naïve and dated hero of *Uncle Tom's Cabin*, whom contemporary American blacks have made a symbol for conscious complicity with the power of the whites.

[5]'*L'ultima arma del patriarcato è la violenza*' in *Paese Sera*, 14 September 1976.

note that men occasionally[6] resort to violence against women. Who would contest this and who does not know why? Is it a reason for sullenly refusing to share responsibilities? A crudely alarmist and partial interpretation of this problem only adds one absurdity to another.

It is therefore insulting and ridiculous to generalize that *all* women are somehow or other (I quote Signora Maraini): 'raped, beaten, killed, brutalized by men and not vice versa'.

It is equally incorrect to claim that in every instance 'women participate in violence, certainly, but as victims. Which sets them on a very different level from that of the brute beasts.'

Shabby conclusions based on meretricious premisses. There is something frankly embarrassing in hearing a writer of Dacia Maraini's reputation and influence advising women, as a panacea for their 'ambiguous status', to take up action that doesn't even rate as original. (Lysistrata, the first 'dairymaid' to go on strike, advocated this method with more wit and for a worthier cause – that of peace.) Listen to this:

'Women will have to start organizing methods and rules for resistance and in defence of their bodies. Hitherto women have had no choice but to surrender them as public or private property. From now on they must fight not to give their bodies at all, restoring through collective work their dignity as complete and independent human beings.'

Setting aside the dry and crypto-religious tone of

[6]Our expert reckons on a rape every three minutes. True, this is in the USA: it seems a lot by our standards! However, one only needs a pocket calculator to work out that these figures (if correct) break down to a rhythm of 0·000002 rapes per day per head of population. A modest ratio, in fact, if one takes into account the pressures of supply and demand . . .

these exhortations, wouldn't they in any case bewilder those Italian women who perhaps still remember their experience of Mussolini's 'dignity of work'. The women of the Fascist era did not find themselves more liberated than the men!

Actually women have had the measure of Dacia Maraini's refrain for some considerable time. Most of them heard the same old song from their mother's lips.

'You are unfortunate enough to have been born a woman,' wails Dacia. 'Men are stronger than you. But you can make up for the curse of destiny by means of devious subtlety and trickery. Learn how to lie! Pretend to be dutiful and attentive so as to get your husband gradually at the mercy of your whims and wishes. If you know how to use your weakness as complaint and turn his strength into fear of you, the game you are playing against man will finally be turned to your advantage. If you are exceptionally skilful in these deceptions, your natural enemies, men, will all be induced, one by one to serve your ambitions and sacrifice themselves to your interests. You will become all-powerful, surrounded by a tribe devoted to your service. Your born masters shall become your subjects.'

But if they knew how to look around them, even the most innocent little girls would soon realize that the old women whispering these fatal doctrines to them were really witches. And they'd also see that even the biggest, strongest and most frightening men are afraid of us – kind, sweet little women that we are . . .

They prefer to expose themselves to the hazards of war, sail single-handed through storms, play roulette, gamble on the Stock Exchange, catch the clap and lose their reputations, rather than brave our nagging and complaining, our tears and hysterical ailments, rather than talk to us or try to tell us their point of view and get us to share their dreams.

These fine fellows would really like to have us as comrades-in-arms, but we do not relish adventure, we cling only to security.

We do our best to make them as homeloving and sly as ourselves: with no success! We find them capable of every audacity when they want to run away from us; of every folly in order to dissipate the boredom we inspire in them by demanding our rights; of every evasion in order to escape from our sanctimonious domesticity; of every recantation so as not to incur our reproaches; of every cowardice so as to avoid seeing us really suffer.

On the subject of cowardice: won't any of those judges contradict me here – the ones who daily pass ever-harsher sentences upon rapists for the very good reason that these magistrates of a legislature renowned for its male pride are simply too scared of exposing themselves to the wrath of feminists utterly obsessed with rape?

I hear no protest either from the men who hypocritically applaud the worst lunacies of some of these same feminist extremists, not because they are sincerely convinced that the women are right, but because it's the current rage in smart circles to support Women's Lib.

It has now reached the stage where no man careful of his reputation would dare make the least casual criticism of even the most dubious Women's Lib slogan or of the most blatant misrepresentation by which this new militancy fudges its statistics. And no writer (if born afflicted with member between legs) who wants to keep a publisher writes one quarter of what I have just said.

Do *you* know any men who let themselves go enough to talk freely and openly about women? You can hold forth about Americans, Russians, Chinese, Zulus, Jews, Arabs, capitalists, the working classes, Martians, all right! No risk involved. But women, no thanks! Too much of a vexed question.

You'll think I'm exaggerating, as ever. Men don't really take feminists seriously.

That's very possible. But I regret it, for I'd like every man to take every woman seriously. Which means I'd like a man to be concerned with seeing a woman's reality, rather than taking offence at her myth.

To make this wish come true, maybe the word feminist should henceforth apply only to a woman who helps men understand women better instead of denoting one whose tirades and tittle-tattle hinder the advance of such understanding.

Above all, the word woman should never be associated with the word *power*. For all power, as Jean-Paul Sartre says, is evil.

So let woman cease dreaming of power which would make her even more incomprehensible and frightening than she already is! And instead of degrading her intelligence by using trickery, pretence and traditional wiles which perpetuate fear, let her stop being a disease to be suffered by men.

II. Opening

Gradual shift of the desert

'I loved you at the expense of others: I did not love you,' Nitya Phenkun makes her siren sister say in *Written on the entrance to a sandy harbour.*

This siren has our voice. All of us are wreckers.

What we call love is a mystifying song. In it we lament our solitude, but not so as to seek new companions. What we want is for another lost traveller to be washed ashore upon our island and to remain with us for a lifetime.

We offer him nothing. We expect nothing of him. What, anyway, can naked swimmers barter? Uncooked shellfish. Wild fruits. One cannot cultivate a beach.

Anyhow, perhaps there are other islands where solitaries like ourselves are languishing. But what language would we use to address them?

We only know how to sing out of tune. Because we whisper 'I love you,' we can no longer say 'I like you.'

Siren captain, your male voice hails me . . . Strange decoy! You are telling me: 'I love only you.' And I am supposed to board this ship. To be loved requires only a little faith.

So my lover, am I your only interest? That's because you need to believe it. And you doubt whether anyone but myself is interested in you. You rely on my faith and make me rely on your doubt.

Love song, you lie! And you too, its singer! You want me to be obsessed with you alone because you are your own sole obsession. But if others cannot win your love, I too shall lose it.

Every involvement costs one dear – in deception, solitude, boredom.

Would you make me pay such a price, if you knew how to love me? Would you deprive me of another love? Would you cheat me out of other lovers? Would you be hurt by the pleasure and interest they gave me? Would you be jealous of my happiness and their beauty?

You talk in order to keep at a distance those who might talk to us. You think you can love me at everyone's expense: so you love me at ours.

I'd understand you better if you were happy that others made me happy. I'd love you more if you loved everyone I loved. My body would be closer to yours if you came whenever someone made me come.

Our species, born to enjoy communal hunting in forests and singing in townships, is moving towards the desert. What's the good of populating this earth if each of us today only knows how to communicate with one other person?

We marry so as to have at least one ally, but also because we think ourselves incapable of making others. We breed children so that someone will need us. No matter who we marry, however, no matter what child we have: we are all made of the same human stuff as dreams. We could give ourselves an infinite family and as many lovers as we have friends. But for that we'd need to dare to live passionately. Alas, fear has been the sole passion of our lives! We fly towards our one true love just as hermits of bygone days take to the desert to escape life.

Around and within us loneliness and sadness rule. The desert is advancing. The desert rises like a huge sea of dust. We become its grains heaped together yet separate. O my lover, do you really want me to be an empty beach for you? Do you want to lose yourself wandering along my shores, seeing only your own footprints? Won't you be afraid there in my domain, when night falls?

Don't you understand that you don't only need me: you need a group of like-minded people. And *I* want to be in this varied world of space and time. I wish to limit no one. Nor can I be a certainty. Uniqueness is no more certain than eternity.

Nowhere is there a siren alone. Every siren has a mortal sister who knows other songs than hers.

I am not an island, my lover. I am not your island. It is easier to dispossess others of me than to possess me.

You say I am all you need. But no one is satisfied with anything or anybody.

There is no happy isolation. Every island is deserted. Every siren weeps because she can only be loved by one castaway at a time. When she stops playing upon her legend and is silent, she dreams of having legs to open to whoever sings to her.

III. Transfinite Love

The battle of the bodies

Has anyone ever seen an atom smile? Can one imagine entropy indulging in a pun? Or space-time playing a practical joke to convulse a nebula? One can't hope for anything of that sort: the universe is incorrigibly serious.

We who watch this dour brewer of quanta; we who make soundings of this deep yet not so radiant father; we who listen to the pulse of this unimpulsive recluse – we are funnier by far.

Is that so? Well, let's first have the arguments in our favour.

Since *we* are capable of finding this universe itself funny, the humour probably stems from us. We are doubtless alone in possessing wit. And if we didn't exist for the sake of finding comedy where there is none, there would be no humour anywhere. The silence of outer space has urgent need of us.

For instance, deprived of our gaze, Nature would have had a hard time discovering her own rules. Without our sense of geometry she would not know her measurements – hips, waist, bust. Without our sense of delicacy she would not know how to express them. Space might be curved without anyone realizing. Without Einstein the movement of the stars would continue to obey Newtonian laws, and without Nils Bohr the molecules would still be wondering whether God or the devil made them.

Another example: our thinkers had difficulty formulating the following 'Three Commandments of Matter':

(1) One lives because of the impossibility of dying.

(2) One dies only according to rule.

(3) Everything not forbidden is compulsory.

Anyone familiar with elementary particles or the behaviour of living organisms knows that the above are not just pleasant witticisms. Muons and their second cousins in the lepton family behave in just this way. And it is also precisely that existence which the amoeba knows.

The amoeba alone? No sooner does one start thinking about this than doubts creep in. Do we ourselves, by any chance – complex and highly developed beings that we are, freed by mind from the fatality of matter – still obey the same principles? That seems less of a laughing matter!

What use is our humanity then? If we cannot die when we wish, in the way we like; if while awaiting our fate we have to go down every one-way street and follow it until we are shown the exit preordained for our eternal rest – what is left of that personal dignity which we hear so much about? We are not free individuals but the playthings of circumstances beyond our control. Chance and necessity, which governed our entry into this world will continue to rule our lives, without our having a say in the matter.

If this is really life, one might as well die!

Ah no, I was forgetting: we do not have the right to die ... On the face of it, we only have duty – in the forms required by authority and the law. A citizen or a believer dies when society decrees or his God allows. No sooner, no later. Living and dying are obligatory.

Then who gives the orders? God? Society? Does someone reign over the life and death of protons, neutrons and electrons? Who? The God of protons? Multinational electrons? The ruling party of neutrons? If any of this were the case, it would be self-evident: but it isn't.

Wait: there is one difference between the world of

matter and ourselves. Matter has no more choice than we, but *it* doesn't obey choices made by others.

If an atom has a 'fate', that fate is an inherent one: the logical internal and external result of its structure. It is not programmed by an outside will.

An electron does not circle a nucleus because richer, more aristocratic and influential electrons have decided that its circle is 'good for it' (and for them!) It does not function because it believes what they say. It does not accelerate through jealousy or ambition. It does not crawl along out of fear. So why does it run?

First of all, it does not run, but advances to its own rhythm. If it moves, that's because somehow it is 'made that way'. It is in motion because such motion is necessary. And if it, rather than another electron, has started this movement, that's because it is better able to complete it. It is content because it does everything of which it is capable.

We are not at all like atoms or stars. We are actually far less free than they. Far worse off – or far more stupid.

No electron would let another electron choose its films or reading matter for it, ban its erotic cinema, make it ashamed of its homosexuality, interfere with its masturbation and instil in it a disgust for extra-marital love. If an electroligarchy tried to compose such limits upon the energy/mass relationships governing other electroproles, revolution would take place within matter itself. The electroproles of all countries would unite! The electropower workers would switch off the electricity. And the electrocrats drunk with domination and thirsting for profits could do nothing except spin in outer darkness.

So is man, the intelligent, the master of critical humour, the crafty observer of the universe, going to let himself be tyrannized more easily than the last of the quarks? Are we less worthy of respect than the meanest neutrino?

Since they get on so much better than we do, how did these minute entities learn the art of politics?

I say 'art', not science. Science has brought only political confusion. It has reached the stage where we wonder if it really concerns us at all. Us, meaning the masses, the pupils, the governed – the parameters of equation, to whom the values of unknown quantities and the positions of the variables are never revealed.

With whom does the power of revelation lie? With mathematicians, teachers, computer programmers, statisticians, economists – those who have the answers. Men of power, in other words.

What then is the difference between their natures and ours? There must be one, otherwise why would we find ourselves numbered among the rank and file, while they are on the other side, sorting us out with ease and authority?

Let us, like the physicists, look for the causes of this discrimination and the laws behind this one-sided activity. Let us be calm and objective, not trusting in appearances. Let us put the mighty and ourselves under the microscope and take a look. The basic differences between us should be glaringly obvious.

And yet they aren't so at all! The anatomy, histology and physiology of the organisms we were once ready to think superior do not reveal any hereditary superiority. The brains of Sacco and Vanzetti were no different from those of their judges and even that of their executioner. And there is every good reason to suppose that the grey matter of the Italian magistrates who burned *Last Tango in Paris* would show neither more nor less complexity than that of Bernardo Bertolucci, the film's director.

Yet one of these men has the right to dispose of

another's life. One of them can stifle an artist's work. Does this seem fair?

What do electrons do then to prevent any of their number making the others' existence miserable?

Don't you know? Try to think, observe them more closely. They stay together. They don't get jealous or doublecross each other. What do they seek? They seek tirelessly to journey together.

It is true that like us they never manage to write, touch each other, understand one another. Yet their *desire* to draw closer is undiminished. I really believe they love each other.

Why can electrons love where we can't? Perhaps because they are only bodies. Perhaps bodies alone know how to love.

Men have forgotten they are bodies. 'They' have made them forget. The Church, of course, but not only the Church. The State is based on denial of the body; it has only been able to establish its power over bodies which have been constrained, appropriated, drained of all private desire and consciousness of individuality: those of soldiers, workers, prisoners, believers, ignoramuses and husbands.

Must one wait for political might or ecclesiastical pestilence to free those whom they have traditionally dominated? The question is meaningless. No past freedom, granted by authority, can become a future freedom. The only possible freedom lies in a variety of spontaneous acts which at a given moment are carried out by bodies animated by one desire.

Any act is within our grasp, however, as soon as our desire is stronger than our fear of power.

Restoring the possibility of freedom to the enslaved thus formulates a militant restitution of the desire.

The consciousness of the desire gives one the wish to fight. And 'he alone deserves freedom and life who has to win them daily'. (Goethe) Freedom can only be gained by physical struggle.

May the hereditary instincts imprinted upon my genes inspire me finally to fight! May you lead me with all my companions in desire towards 'a free land where I shall stand among a free race. To every fleeting moment I can then say, Stop, you are so beautiful!' (Goethe)

Yes, of all the men and women I desire – none of you are replaceable. I cannot do without the nearest or farthest of you. That is why I do not want to let you die.

I too have lived for you, am living for you . . .

If I were to die before desiring you, before you desired me, the whole world would be changed by that, just as though an atom were missing from it . . . If my father were to die . . . or the men who made me suffer . . . or the women I've made cry . . . or the sailor who rescued me . . . or the fishermen who fed me . . . or the doctors who healed me . . . or the inventors whose inventions have carried me to all the corners of the earth . . . or the seers who have opened my eyes . . . And if the eyes of my lovers had remained closed . . . If the war had gone on longer . . . If those who taught me the word freedom had not been born . . .

I've been free, thanks to them all. And am. As you are.

Unlike the electron, I do dream. But I don't expect my dreams to become a reality. I choose my life: I chose life. I love this world, enjoy space, live out time. I fight on physically, I use my allotted span. I am not giving myself back to eternity.

I know no fear or hope and thus am free.

You too! Because, like the electron, you have nothing to fear. And because, like the electron, you have nothing to hope for.

You have everything to wish for! To whoever desires without fear or hope all things are possible.

The single question

'Come on!' you may say, 'what's this philosophy you're talking about? Are you by any chance taking yourself a bit too seriously? What needs or hidden frustrations does your system answer?'

No philosophy gives an answer to anything or anybody. A philosophy is nothing but a way of asking questions. The good philosophy is the one which asks the good questions. A philosophy that wanted to be absolutely useful would no doubt ask only a single question and thus avoid our wasting our lives resolving problems that don't really concern us.

I do not know if eroticism, or my eroticism, is a philosophy, but I know it has this sort of usefulness. It asks of conventional morality this single question: must a man make love with only one woman, or a woman with just one man?

You'll retort: 'Isn't eroticism more the art of relationships, the game of situations, the science of positions?'

Of course it is, and today everyone thinks himself more erotic than his neighbour. Why then does the erotic continue to shock and why does it still cause fear?

Eroticism provokes the greatest scandal not by giving us an occasional sexual bonus but in making us wonder whether or not one person alone can provide the answer to our every desire.

Certainly this question is scandalous, like all the other essential ones society doesn't allow us to ask aloud. Society doesn't allow it because the whole object of authority is to provide its own answers for every question. And our duty as citizens is to believe collectively in what authority tells us. Morality, the family structure, and social order are based upon our lack of curiosity and on our trust.

With what dogma does society answer our need for knowledge?

'Do you want everything? Well, your spouse will be everything to you. Your universe. You shall have no other companion in life, no other sexual partner or lover. Till you die, this one being shall for you embody all others. And in this world of mutiplicity you shall be eternally alone with him or her. If you think differently, you'll be beyond the moral pale of your country and times.'

Since this is how things are, why are we simultaneously and constantly harangued about the rights of man: freedom of thought, expression, association, choice? Why are we assured that a political regime is loathsome if it denies such freedom to its meanest citizen? Or is perpetual restriction the supreme law of societies because it is the law of matter?

But does Nature have laws?

'Opinion is the colour, opinion the sweetness, opinion the bitterness . . . In reality nothing exists other than the atom and the void.'

Did a contemporary materialist say that? No, a very ancient one, Democritus, that precursor of scientific objectivity whom Plato so hated that he preferred to maintain that the former had never existed. Like so many others, this was a vain ploy concocted from religious fervour! Twenty-five centuries later learning is still not possible other than on the assumption of Democritus.

What do the makers of civil and moral laws matter? Greater or lesser Platos, who only want us to be shadows across the walls of their churches or their barracks, continue dictating 'opinions' which are less real than the void and imposing upon us duties which our atoms cannot accept.

Our atoms, meaning our physical nature, which makes us tend towards multiple and changeable relationships, give us the taste for complex and varied experiences. Under the scientist's microscope atom does not cease interacting with atom in perpetual motion. If a relationship is formed that renders further, different combinations impossible, the structure formed is short-lived. The only unions to survive, perfect themselves and flourish are those able to evolve by attracting other elements, whether in order to try out new pairings or to create threefold, fourfold or still more complicated groups.

Human beings, it will be said, are more than atoms, precisely because, whether Democritus liked it or not, they are capable of 'opinions'. Very well, but let us go back to the subject of 'rights' and ask what an opinion is worth if it is not free.

Whenever we deprive ourselves of the pleasures of getting to know one more lover; whenever we think we are wrong to have several lovers and justify ourselves by saying that we love each in a different way; whenever we draw a factitious line between friendship and love – are we proving we are free, or simply renouncing the right to enjoy our mortal lives as we wish? What shadowy reward do we want?

It seems that by being docile we gain a soul. Really, what a nice asset this marvellous soul is, which isolates us so totally.

Unhappiness is our presumed fate. There is no unhappiness in the real world any more than there is tragedy, for reality has no fate. There can be tragedy only where behaviour and concepts stem from faith.

Our life is tragic because we believe that somewhere outside ourselves an answer to the question of our uniqueness can be found. And because we believe there is no answer to the questions posed by our diversity.

Perhaps being happy is nothing more than being delivered from a faith. We suffer less when we occupy ourselves with questions than when we worry about answers.

Throughout our lives, every friend asks us questions we cannot adequately answer. Throughout our sex lives, every lover creates desires in us which he or she cannot fully gratify. As long as we have hearts, every love issues a challenge which our fidelity cannot cope with.

If these questions, desires and challenges are to mean anything to us, let us know how to have more than one friend, let us give more than one lover hope, let us be faithful to more than one love.

On being a jellyfish

If someday I could be reincarnated, I should like to be reborn a jellyfish.

I don't simply have this dream because I am haunted by the desire for a submarine existence, nor because floating between lichens and hammer-head sharks would necessarily be less dangerous than manoeuvring between piratical publishers and phoney film producers.

There are other reasons why the jellyfish's destiny attracts me. It is in fact the only creature I know of to be born female, turn hermaphrodite, and finish up male. It thus has experience of three sexes during its lifetime.

One can say that men and women have a hard time understanding each other because the thoughts and feelings of either sex remain hopelessly obscure to the other. True, but I might just as well maintain that women do not get on so marvellously among themselves. Nor are men any more tolerant towards one another.

Inflexibility rather than variability is the worst obstacle to peace of mind. What makes for impatience is the prospect of never changing character, situation, mentality or skin. What makes one hate another is anger at not being able to become that other.

Greek mythology is proof of the antiquity of the mystery. Everybody knows the legend of Tiresias, that soothsayer who, while wandering about in search of omens, encountered two serpents making love. Through embarrassment, ill-luck or pure stupidity, he parted the amorous ophidians with blows of his staff. Most of us would do the same, even today, if we met a boy and girl rolling around naked in the middle of the street.

Zeus used to have whims and prejudices which would vary day by day. On this occasion, either because the live show pleased him or because the two snakes were old friends of his , the spoilsport's intervention really got on his nerves. With just a snap of his fingers he turned Tiresias into a woman.

According to contemporary tradition such a devaluation was in itself officially considered a nasty trick to play on anybody.

By his action the god showed yet again that he did not know a great deal about his creation. Some years later, in fact, Tiresias, whose life had been full of ups and downs, heard Zeus calling him once more. He wanted Tiresias to help him settle an argument with Hera, his divine wife.

As usual their bone of contention was crude enough: the king of the gods and his wife were arguing about whether the man or the woman experienced most pleasure from lovemaking. Tiresias, with firsthand experience of both sexes, was the very person to enlighten them.

He did not hesitate: the woman's pleasure in orgasm, he revealed, was *nine times stronger* than the man's. Zeus thanked him for his opinion by turning him back into a man. This time the punishment was harsh!

Why nine times, though, rather than eight or ten? This no version of the story explains. Tiresias was simply more precise than our current sexologists.

Unfortunately his source of information and system are not generally accessible. Trans-sexuals, i.e. those who physically change sex through surgery, are not impartial judges.

Really being a woman, then a real man (or vice versa) would be quite another matter. I'm sure the history of the world would be different if such changes were possible. Most of our misdeeds spring from our wanting to be something else. If we could be sure in advance of becoming our opposites the prospect would probably have the effect – if it did not ensure our eternal happiness – of making us rather more cautious . . .

A friend, a militant feminist, has read the foregoing and is protesting about it. In her opinion such evolution should only be one-way: everyone must start off as men, since men must be forced to become women. Why? To punish them! Zeus is not dead.

I've already said that these vindictive politics are alien to me. I have never felt unhappy about being a woman. So I do not regard femininity as a punishment. If I could be reborn I would prefer to be a woman rather than a man. But I still maintain that being able to be both would be best of all. And all things considered, not one after the other: both at once.

The most desirable lot is that of the jellyfish – hermaphroditism. That would once and for all resolve our futile struggles for precedence. The world would be more pleasant for all if everyone were of the same sex.

Someone will grumble that these dreams are absurd, as far removed from philosophy as from science. But is it certain that philosophy and science are enough to satisfy us? A need exists in us which is more insubstantial, irrational and impracticable still. The desperate urgency of love.

The experience of true love is, on our planet, as unlikely an event as being reborn a jellyfish. There is no more real love on earth than there are true hermaphrodites. Only one sure reality exists within and between human beings, that of the void.

The same apparently impassable distance separating the stars also separates men. However, elementary particles by the million meet and merge, while heavenly bodies gravitate in a harmonious order. Why can't men?

Atoms and stars understand each other because they

move. The secret of their contentment is called motion. Motion results from space and time.

We too have this potential within us. Life and thought are possible because time fills the voids.

If time did not let the gene become a cell and the cell a changing body, the earth would be lifeless. If the idea did not have time to form, the reflection to mature, the intelligence to develop, life would not transcend the animal level.

It has taken millions of years for the universe to learn to live, millions of years for animate matter to learn to think. So let's have a day of grace beforc we despair. More than a few millennia, perhaps, and then we might end up learning to love.

My lovers' wives

Most of the time I don't fill the wives of my lovers with anxiety. Sometimes they simply pretend to know nothing. Often though, they deliberately treat me very nicely, seeking my company and even my friendship. So it seems to me that I cause women no more alarm than I do men.

If married women are so unperturbed by my relationships with their husbands, it's probably because they know – through intuition rather than research – that I make love out of pleasure. They would only turn against me if I were to threaten them in the really private area of wedlock, that of money matters.

The material interest at the heart of the institution of matrimony cannot under any circumstances stand competition. All else is flexible and accommodating, on condition of course that domestic and social appearances are preserved. My real good fortune is simply due to the fact that pleasure doesn't interest 'deceived' wives.

It goes without saying that none of the women who are like me is ever 'deceived'. When I make love to the husbands or lovers of these women, I am giving *them* pleasure at the same time. Yet these sensations and feelings too, for those not bold enough to experience them, are without interest . . .

The interests of the average married woman are defined without the slightest reference to pleasure. They consist for her solely of belonging, being looked after and being protected.

Belonging or being 'placed' means to be assured of a recognized social status: such status makes her, she believes, respectable and, she hopes, enviable. Being looked after consists of being housed and clothed and of having well-dressed children. Protection, finally, means that throughout her entire life she is spared the worry of thinking for herself or taking her own decisions and risks. Should her parents be dead or elderly, one person alone can provide her with these particular long-term services – a husband.

You think I've been describing machinations and customs only found among the rich and that working-class marriages aren't like that? Well unfortunately working-class households, too, whenever they get the chance, are just as possessive as those of the privileged. They fall under petticoat rule just like those of the well-heeled, are quite as bourgeois as bourgeois homes, and are certainly even richer in prejudices than those of the upper classes. In the world of matrimony there is no class struggle, only privileged quarrelling.

For a great many women fear of losing their husbands is thus merely confused with the fear of no longer enjoying the commodities and things which come (and go) with having a husband. It's no accident that a married woman's most frequently used words are 'in our house' or 'at home'. The wrappings have very soon acquired more importance for her than the contents, in the same way as dressing up comes to seem more sensual to her than nakedness.

Houses and clothes wear out, however. Marriage seen as fine clothes or a house in which you live alone together in time undergoes the same deterioration as gilt belts and plaster façades. And the women who seek refuge in such things sooner or later have to cling to the wreckage of security, to bonds that are in tatters and which they will admit are more and more frayed as life slips by.

Some start out saying: 'All I ask is that he isn't unfaithful,' then compromise with the less ambitious wish: 'He can do what he likes, provided I don't hear about it!' Then the climb-down is steeper: 'Provided he comes and eats at home each evening!' 'On condition that he shows up now and again!' 'As long as he doesn't make me lose face in front of my friends!' Until the inevitable: 'Provided that he gives me enough money for my upkeep and the children's.'

If the normal course of a marriage is destined to work out this way, why not begin at once with the end? And for the traditional nuptials, the organ music and incense substitute a simple and honest hire purchase agreement? One would stop pretending one marries for love and would frankly accept that the partnership is for the purpose of keeping shop, doing the cooking, wiping the arses of lawful offspring with the latest coloured kleenex, and reconciliation after an exchange of bitter reproaches and blows?

Isn't this actually the typical family situation? It was the introduction of the illusion of love into this materialistic arrangement which distorted everything. Since we are aware that the love we profess is a myth and our hypocrisy a sickness, let us have done with these idle dreams once and for all!

The snag is that there is only one sure way of destroying a collective myth and curing one's own personal hallucinations: confronting them with realities. We will therefore free ourselves from the myth of love and the mental disorders it breeds only if we succeed in inventing a real love, a realistic love.

Such a love would claim to be no more than a new pleasure, a new freedom for all.

The freedom which contemporary men and women can show themselves capable of and must learn to use lies in acknowledging that pleasure has positive worth, and that to seek pleasure is the mark of intelligence. Our mystical illusions have never been free: they have been forced upon us. Our economic and political disillusions have not been intelligent: we were mistaken. We are free to change habits and struggle against ignorance. Freedom is the narrow path along which desire leads to understanding.

For as long as mind and body let themselves be enslaved, desire can breed only myths.

But no ontological definition of freedom exists other than 'the possibility of knowing everything'. And basically this is also perhaps the ultimate essence of pleasure. Whoever knew everything would doubtless be utterly happy. Ignorance, doubt, faith and hope are what makes us suffer most.

Yet since we shall never be completely free nor ever know everything, our apprenticeships can be realized in practice only by tentative mutations of desire – so that what we learn perpetually increases our taste for the unknown and our wish to go still further.

Being dead to desire is not to seek to know anything more and wanting to keep what one assumes is one's place. To stop desiring is one particularly painful way of dying young.

To live is to refuse to stop along the way, whether at the birth of wisdom or action, while remaining aware that one doesn't exactly know what one is doing nor really where one is going. It does not mean, as sometimes stated, going right on to the end – for there is no end. It is enough to be convinced of one single law, that of the atom, which is ours also: the only real way of going astray is to stop.

This is the only real loss too. We lose only those we allow to continue without us. And we are lost only to those who let us go onward without them.

So the best way never to lose is always to love. Love, the true love which still doesn't exist and which only eroticism can make a reality, will be something that deprives us of nothing and separates us from nobody.

This passion, this reason will reveal to us that even change, sharing and absence, are linked. And thus we will finally know that, however paradoxical it may seem, to love is not to live in fear of loss.

Today no other credible ideal presents itself to mankind as a replacement for its dead myths. Eroticism is the only modern rationale we can find through which to understand one another, whatever our race: the only way we can together be impatient for tomorrow, revel in our differences and communicate our dreams.

Really the only way? What actually are the alternatives? Eternal life, moneymaking, war only tempt the mentally retarded. The exploration of space, it is true, could also reconcile mankind and help it progress, but no doubt this won't really get under way until the day after tomorrow. Television, which for the moment constitutes the one universal passion, will soon, in its turn, be an antiquated craze. As for political ideology, we are no longer capable of inventing anything new, nor even of exercising choice. So I honestly do not see any way out of our current mental sloth except through the invention of another *kind* of love.

Is this future common cause vaguely glimpsed by those of my lovers' wives who are not jealous? No doubt they are already aware that I am taking nothing from them. Perhaps they even understand that from the arms of the men they love my own arms reach out to them.

When they are bold enough to put their hands in mine an age-old fear is overcome. The discovery of a new world begins.

A dentist told me one day: 'Existence, for those who don't like to suffer, can be disagreeable. Those who find pleasure in suffering lead a more enjoyable life.'

This man was too unimaginative for me to regard this maxim as a joke. So I never again let him inside my mouth. Or anywhere else. A gynaecologist once informed me that one should never introduce into the vagina what one would not put into one's mouth and I suppose the reverse is equally true.

What sort of philosophy was my dentist trying to convey with his gibberish? The golden rule of the Masochists' Friendly Society? Or simply Christian morality? To clear up this point I'll ask the representatives of this morality a question which, given their charity, ought not to offend them: why does the Catholic faith consider suffering an investment whose dividends consist of years of eternal life?

After all, nothing obliges the Church to try and pass off suffering as a virtue. If it took note of the fact that human life is full of misfortune and found no cause for rejoicing therein, that would be understandable. Buddhism is founded on a similar acknowledgment. The second of its three assumptions is *Dukhang*, meaning: 'Everything suffers' (the first being *Aniccang*, 'Everything passes', and the third, *Anatta*, 'There is no soul'). This said, Buddha did not start preaching that one should look on suffering as a blessing from heaven. Still less did he think that one should really work at suffering. Quite the contrary: after an unsatisfactory experience of asceticism had left him frail and feeble, he was interested only in finding ways to avoid suffering.

Only the Holy Fathers of the Roman Catholic Church have had the bright idea of advising us to suffer as much as possible for our own good.

This brainwave founded a whole school of thought. The entire Western tradition is just a chorus of exhortations to mortification, privation and austerity. Let's skip mysticism, a boring and somewhat ridiculous subject, and confine ourselves to looking at literature, morality, the education of the family, and politics. In these areas the prevailing note is one of gloom and misery.

Should we not wonder whether the human race is predominantly masochistic? Psychology in its existing form has not succeeded in telling us, and it's a pity. Our tormentors would play less easily upon our ideas and feelings if we ourselves were a little less ignorant about what we thought and felt. Once again it appears that our abject condition results from our lack of knowledge.

If we want to move from a life-style which hurts us to a more pleasurable existence, it's a matter of some urgency that we become better informed.

As sex is the main source of pleasure, it follows that sex information is the most necessary if our civilization is to progress.

It might seem that this area is already well covered. Bookshops are overstocked with sex education manuals. There are an increasing number of magazines and periodicals devoted entirely to sexuality. Even the lesser women's magazines allot an ever-increasing number of pages to agony columns and advice on sexual problems. In short, as the prudes complain, it does seem as if sex is everywhere.

If this is the case, why do I continue to receive an incredible number of letters in which bewildered men and women ask me whether oragenital contact is likely to poison those who practise it, or if a man who sodomizes a woman is a pederast?

Since these people write to me seeking advice, they

must on some occasion have read something I've written and probably too some sample of the didactic-erotic literature I have just mentioned. It does seem that such reading has made little impression upon them. Conclusion: the printed word is not a satisfactory source of sexual information.

What remains? Image and sound, of course. Artwork, photography, theatre, cinema, dance, song, music can stir up our desires. Is it absolutely certain that they can teach us to enjoy life more fully?

To put it another way, is there nothing left for us but the cynicism of my dentist?

Whenever I meet some successful director, some beautiful woman, some talented young person who has everything going for them and is still not happy, I really begin to wonder whether the destiny of every animal is to suffer and if it isn't utopian to try to prevent their doing so.

However, I haven't yet succeeded in denying my thirst for knowledge. I'd like to know why we are so ill-made . . . So for the hundredth time I question an attractive woman: 'Do you think you are attractive? – Yes. – Are you proud of your beauty? – Yes. – Then why do you hide your breasts? – Because it'd be wrong to show them. – Why wrong? – Because it's not decent. – What do you mean, not decent? – People would think I was a whore. – Don't you like being desired? – Yes. – In that case, why do everything you can in order not to be desired? – Because that sort of thing just isn't done. – Must you do only what others do? – I didn't say that. – But whenever you want to make love with a man, do you do it? – Of course not. – What's stopping you? Are you afraid of your husband? Or of what people might say? – No, nobody would know. – Then why don't you do it? – One doesn't do everything one wants to do. – If you were to indulge your wish, would it harm anyone? –

Maybe not, but the guilt would make *me* unhappy. – Why would you feel guilty? – Because I'd have behaved badly. – Well then, behave badly! That way you can regret, suffer and weep your fill, since you like that so much! – What are you talking about? Like *what* so much? – Being unhappy. – Are you crazy? I'm not a masochist!'

Pointless conversation. Futile investigation. Useless inquiry. The desire for knowledge prompts my questions but doesn't give me an answer. Knowledge never provides answers, it only poses new questions. Only the ignorant claim to know the truth.

Why then are the ignorant and the believers, whom God has taught everything, still so miserable? Is it because their God came down to Earth to learn in their place and left them nothing to discover? Or because he did not think of teaching them joy? Perhaps he just didn't have time: he died too soon.

One must continue to ask questions and go on being dissatisfied with the answers. Above all we must stop looking to others, or Another, for all the answers. We have to learn to be alone in the world. Learn to be alone without weeping . . .

When we learn that, maybe we'll also learn how to laugh. To laugh alone at our mortal destiny. To laugh with others at our desire to escape death.

Then we shall forget that once we only knew how to suffer and cause suffering. We shall not remember former ties which hurt us, former words which hurt others, former stars which made us leave those we loved. We shall have new dreams. We shall awake to new suns. Together we shall wait for the day to dawn, we who each morning were only able to wait for nightfall. We shall be new-born.

An end to No Entry

The part of town I live in is like every other: its most obvious ornaments consist of traffic signs. No Parking, No Entry, One-Way Street. One road, though, is rather different. It is short but wide: four vehicles can drive down it abreast. In spite of such ease of access this road has always, for as long as I've known it, been a one-way street. At least that was the intention of the authorities, who put signs to the effect at either end. But drivers are of a different opinion: every day countless cars drive down either way, blissfully ignorant of the threatened penalties.

The public's behaviour intrigues me for two reasons. Firstly, no one dreams of infringing the rules in any of the other one-way streets in my neighbourhood. The small road to which I refer is the only one where municipal regulations are regarded as unimportant.

My second reason for surprise is this: the street runs right past a police station! 'Past' is perhaps a misnomer: the enormous barrack-like frontage of this police station takes up almost its entire length. This means that hundreds, or maybe thousands, of offenders who drive up it the wrong way every day are doing so under the very noses of the police, who from the doorways and windows of their HQ observe these infringements without lifting a finger to caution or put a stop to them.

For a long time I wondered why these functionaries didn't function, but I never dared ask them. I assumed it was because there were just too many offenders. If only one or two people daily had risked going down the wrong way the guardians of the law would doubtless have stopped and questioned them. Faced with a hundred or a thousand culprits, the long arm of the law would have to let matters drop.

Suddenly the situation has changed. This morning I looked in vain for the red signpost with its white stripe which I've seen for years: it was no longer there. Had someone pulled it down or stolen it? My curiosity finally got the better of my caution. A policeman was strolling along nearby. I asked him what had happened to the sign.

'We withdrew it,' he told me, 'to preserve the dignity of the law. Since no one took any notice of this one-way street, we had to lift the restriction.'

What unlikely miracles, then, may happen in my neighbourhood? Might it by chance become the first in the town (the country, the world?) where democracy is established? For what does democracy mean if not a regime whereby the people make the laws?

When by some strange consensus of opinion drivers agreed that this particular one-way regulation was absurd, and refused to acknowledge it, they certainly acted rebelliously, but was this due to lack of good citizenship or a taste for anarchy? That's hard to believe, because at the very next intersection they dutifully went on turning in the direction the traffic-signs indicated.

In the latter case they accepted that the indication officially marked out served some purpose and extricated them from worse inconvenience. So these individuals were not organized troublemakers, terrorists, rebels against the rule of law, but conscientious citizens who considered they had the right to criticize the law.

The authorities in this case recognized that collective contempt for a bad law renders that law null and void. If this example were unique, however, it would be of no great interest: yet the withdrawal of that small red and white sign is not the only evidence of positive action of this nature. I remember having previously noted (in *The Hypothesis of Eros*, 1974) a statement by General de Gaulle, whose supporters and colleagues refrained from giving it the publicity it deserved (although he was speaking at a Press Conference at the Elysée Palace on 21 February, 1966). The late French President said on that occasion: 'Nothing can be done to enforce a law when it is no longer in line with current opinion, short of amending it . . . So the law must be adapted to new data, failing which, outdated texts devoid of meaning will, if necessary, be mere fodder for the archives, unless violent schism occurs between these obsolete elements and living realities.'

A few years later this kind of thinking was spectacularly reflected by the Bundestag on 7 June 1973, when German MPs decided to abolish all previously existing penalties against pornography in West Germany.

'This step,' explained Schoeller, one of the German legislators, 'is intended to bring the law into line with prevailing customs and morality.' Gerhard Jahn, the Minister of Justice, who introduced the bill, himself justified his action as follows: 'The citizen must be allowed full freedom of choice upon matters of personal sexual conduct. The old penal standards have come to lack credibility and are thus counter-productive.'

Since then, elsewhere in the world, the people's will has brought about a number of reforms which were alien to the authorities – and which would never have been passed by them had not pressure of public opinion forced their hand. In France, for example, first contraception then abortion were legalized. One law changed divorce procedure, because there law and custom had themselves long been divorced. Spouses wishing to end their marriages had had to play-act a 'judicial comedy' to assuage the consciences of various law courts, but the government and Parliament finally recognized that this was prejudicial to 'the dignity of the law', to quote my policeman's phrase. The State therefore resolved to revise the law, in accordance with current morality.

In Italy, likewise, the referendum of May 1974, by which 66 per cent of the population voted in favour of divorce, made a reactionary leadership acknowledge the real will of the country. Contraception had already been legalized by means of a constitutional interpretation which was actually a camouflaged surrender to the people's demands.

Laws which seemed to be rock-solid and likely to last for ever have also surrendered to world-wide ridicule: because of this gradual revolution, homosexuality, adultery, incest, freedom of artistic expression are already causing less alarm.

Yet the oppression of the past remains boundless. In many countries women are far from exercising full and complete freedom of choice as to how many children they want. In order to terminate an unwanted pregnancy, they have to make excuses, get a doctor's permission, and sometimes risk prison. Mechanical or chemical methods of contraception are still often difficult to obtain, especially for young people. In addition, a dubious propaganda campaign of lies disguised as scientific fact is striving to discredit the use of the Pill. Many women dare not take it because they've let themselves be persuaded by establishment doctors that this hormonal method might cause cancers (the opposite has been proved true) or possibly embolisms (no more so than by eating *boeuf bourguignon*).

Demanding the abolition of superannuated laws which cause unhappiness is possible only if we first exercise our right to correct information. The minority governments in power well know that the will of the people would leave them no chance of maintaining their supremacy. Yet this will cannot take shape for as long as the people remain ignorant of the truth. Deception constitutes the main weapon of domination.

We agree to accept bad laws not because we are afraid to rebel, but because we do not know they are bad. The moment we have proof that they are wrong, we are ready for anything. Drivers usually follow one-way systems because they are convinced that without such control, annoying though it may be, urban traffic would be paralysed. But when a restriction is manifestly pointless and unjustifiable, like that imposed upon my little street, they do not respect it. Even the presence of the police in the restricted zone does not intimidate those who are aware of a folly and an injustice.

Most of our sexual taboos are still only accepted by our contemporaries because a huge majority remains unaware of the folly and injustice of these rules. Millions of men and women let themselves be tormented by moral absurdities, social proprieties and legal anachronisms that treat sexual pleasure as an evil, love as a danger and happiness as a reprehensible Utopia. They let this happen because they themselves believe these myths. They believe in them because organized family and State education, aiming to preserve privilege and the status quo, have conditioned them to be credulous and resigned.

Sexual freedom will not be the fruit of violent revolution, any more than human beings will learn to love each other through process of law or the horsewhip. Freedom's apprenticeship and the formation of judgment go hand in hand: intelligence is not divisible.

As long as our species goes on believing that happiness is not possible on this earth and that we must take our chances in the hazards of another life; as long as women go on believing that their fate lies in men's hands and vice versa; as long as men and women imagine that their pleasure rests upon mutual appropriation; as long as couples base their harmony and the length of their relationships upon the care they take to slam the door of jealousy and shut out any casual visitor from their beds; as long as lovers spend more time in careful calculations than bold experiments; as long as the whole world proudly continues 'not wanting to know', life will remain for us what it is at present: a No Entry.

Let us not wait, though, for our leaders to instruct us! Our freedom would not be in their interest. Education is not designed to enable children to become more intelligent, imaginative and enterprising than their parents: the superiority of a younger generation would shame the older one. Old people prefer to be able to say: 'Things were better in our day.' To ensure that things won't be even better tomorrow, the old take care that their descendants are none the wiser than they. Education is a conspiracy destined to perpetuate ignorance.

A new generation thus has the chance to learn only by self-instruction. Official information is guarded jealously. Our only other remaining option is experience.

The first men, those inventors of fire, dancing, kissing, the *soixante-neuf* and the love song, didn't rely solely on their teachers for information: they worked out their ideas for themselves, alone and by chance, through rubbing together pieces of wood or flint, lips and sexes, reeds and dried skins. So let's not be concerned with simply accepting whatever 'sex education' deems fit to tell us. Let us progress tentatively, follow our ideas and whims, refuse to accept any repressive system which prevents true exploration of our bodies and minds. Minds above all!

This true eroticism will evolve one day. The rest will follow, as legislators and police follow when people themselves have a hand in their own destinies. Let us hope that our minds then control our bodies and that our sensuality takes us boldly the wrong way down one-way streets and into No Entry!

Criminal or nymphomaniac?

Medicine and criminology are both fashionable, and this is bad for them and for us since a liking for things in fashion hinders sound judgment.

As a matter of fact, if today it is the done thing to seek medical treatment, it is even more chic to talk about the harm caused by doctors, and their medications. And society has always been torn between fearing criminals and fearing judges. This contradiction is in no small way responsible for society's disorientation, dissatisfaction and ill-functioning. Perhaps these defects are due above all to the fact that we do not really know what should be termed crime and what sickness: so much so that we finally resort to fashion in order to settle the distinction.

In this respect, quite enough controversy has been aroused by the label generally known as 'madness'. In our own era a whole school of anti-psychiatry has based itself upon attacking accepted definitions. The most serious of these psychiatrists have in the last analysis come round to suggesting that no one is mad or, which amounts to the same thing, that we all are. In any given period of history the definition of madness is not an objective, scientific judgment but a majority consensus: in other words, it is yet again a question of fashion. During another era the roles of madness and normality would be reversed.

However widespread this concept, it does not persuade specialists or laymen to tread at all warily. They blithely continue branding those who do not resemble everyone else as abnormal, and if they get the chance, have such people committed or ostracized. If mad people benefit from that tolerance sometimes afforded to artists, it is because art (according to majority opinion) is one madness which excuses all others. Unless, that is, an artist really does draw attention to himself, in which case the age-old question arises: should he be treated like a lunatic or a criminal? Should one feel sorry for him and look after him or, on the contrary, punish him?

The preordained victims of this concern are, of course, the erotic artists, the writers and film-makers who put before the public an image of love for which the public is unprepared. Actually the word 'erotic' has undergone a strange transformation. Previously applied to love poetry, it now no longer means 'amorous' but 'contrary to the general sense of decency'.

I've already taken the opportunity of saying that I found the change a happy one: in fact it brings eroticism back to the realm of art, for all art should be an attack upon established customs. An art that reassures, an art that simply reaffirms its spectators' habitual thinking or their ways of looking is a useless art. Art's real function is to bring new visions into being and to dare men to risk unusual ideas and images.

This function is dangerous. Novelty invariably causes fear and fear incites those who feel it to punitive reactions. Artists will never be safe in the world.

The risks they run vary according to their times. In more extreme times they were hanged or burned. Today they are only sentenced to lesser punishments, they are imprisoned or ruined. Above all, however, people dismiss them and ridicule their creations.

Now I am going to break my rule: as my readers are well aware, I make a point of discussing my own affairs as little as possible. This particular example of society's aggression towards a writer who disturbs it, in fact concerns myself. I've decided to tell the story not because it's alarming, but rather because it's amusing. It does also illustrate quite well the devious way in which people try to make fun of those whom they dare not openly admit to hating.

Some time ago in Paris a 'cocktail-debate' (the very name gives some idea of the concept's snobbery) was organized on the theme of 'Eroticism: Crime or Liberation?' Even the title is revealing! Just like the nature of the organization whose idea it was – The International Society for the Prevention of Crime, founded and run by prominent legal men.

Imagine my surprise on receiving an invitation to this discussion. The reason was that the organizers could think of nothing better than basing their discussion on the following subject: 'Is Emmanuelle a normal or abnormal woman?' Nice, eh? Of course I refused to appear before this 'tribunal' and contented myself with sending a tongue-in-cheek letter which was read out to the learned assembly.

The gist of the letter was as follows:

'I wouldn't know how to contribute to your debate, for I do not know what a *normal* woman or man is. I am not ashamed of such ignorance, for I am in good company. In September 1969 a hundred of the greatest names in world anthropology met at UNESCO in Paris with the purpose of reaching an agreement as to the origin of "modern man" (the latest fashionable terminology for what was once known as homo sapiens). These acknowledged experts couldn't even succeed in defining what man was! They only agreed on one point: as things stand, it is not possible to set down a human norm. A human being defies all classification.

'That was the opinion of scientific men. It obviously isn't the view of legal minds: everything, according to the latter, can and must be categorized. And every individual not conforming exactly to such categories as specified is to be termed abnormal.

'I happen to prefer the ignorance of scientists to the

omniscience of jurists. I also feel more comfortable in the company of the former, which will explain my absence.

'But as you have done me the honour of asking me a question, I'd like your permission to ask you something too.

'First of all, kindly enlighten me on one point: is one born abnormal or does one become so? If one becomes so, does one owe such evolution to the evil natures God has given us or to the evil society in which we have had the bad luck to find ourselves?

'If the desire for loving as much as one wants and as many men and women who seem worth loving, if this desire which you stigmatize as eroticism, seems criminal to you, tell me this; is it innate or acquired? If innate, do you have the right to condemn it any more than obesity, stammering, lameness or colourblindness? If acquired, how can this happen other than through culture? And aren't you claiming to speak in culture's name?

'Yes I know: you don't want others to go beyond the degree of culture you yourselves have attained. And since you personally aren't capable of that kind of love, you forbid it. It is criminal to progress further than you, feel more than you, fuck more than you, think better than you, dare anything other than your hypocritical courage. What you call normal is knowing one's place and keeping to it – that place in all circumstances being some way behind you.

'Ladies and Gentlemen, it's true you aren't judges but criminologists – no, I'm mistaken, you want to invent a form of "criminal prophylaxis". You are health inspectors, with dreams of being doctors, not cops.

'Right, but here's something else you should know. A real doctor doesn't worry about knowing whether his patient is normal or not: he wants to know if the patient is in pain; whether he is threatened with physical decline or death. And he will then try to relieve the suffering, delay the onset of senility and death.

'Does someone who has learned to come more deeply than most suffer? Does anyone capable of loving several men or women simultaneously and of being loved by them suffer? Does someone suffer who has got rid of the agonies and torments of jealousy? Is someone who loves their lover's pleasure suffering? No? Then don't you interfere by trying to cure them.

'It isn't the sick who interest you, though, it's sickness. And in your opinion you've already discovered the name of the illness from which Emmanuelle is suffering: nymphomania!

'Emmanuelle a nymphomaniac? A medical gathering which diagnosed her as one would obviously compensate for the authorities' failure to turn her into a criminal (for the crime of obscenity), or that of the self-righteous and repressed to have her branded as a whore. What a ridiculous enterprise! Especially as the definition of nymphomania, like that of every illness, is that it involves suffering: it is a desperate race for an orgasm that never occurs. Now I didn't think Emmanuelle has made love once in her life without coming. And I don't believe that coming causes her any pain . . .

'So, because I resemble her, I am going to try hard to please you: I'm answering Yes to your question! Emmanuelle is abnormal. She is abnormal in a society where normality means envy, frustration and hate. She is abnormal among people prepared to do without pleasure in order to deprive others of it too. She is abnormal because she wants to change, change herself and her life.

'You, Ladies and Gentlemen of the Jury, are normal. You are the sort who dreamed up stationary planets, hanging for ever from God's finger in the unmoving ether. You refused to believe in Evolution, cursing Darwin after Galileo. You are ashamed of having been algae, amoeba, fish, monkey, before being Man and are terrified at the thought that this mutating animal might yet become something else. To reassure yourselves you have established hereditary rights, conformity, the social and clerical order, the army, religion. To fix humanity within the deadly constancy you dream of, you make use of weight of numbers, force of arms, of laws, and of political and moral force. And yet you're still afraid! All movement seems unnatural to you, although the whole of Nature is always on the move. Your kingdom is not of this earth. Rest there in peace!'

On prostitution

A good deal of my bad reputation is due to the persistence I show in defending prostitutes. I'm sure that self-righteous people would forgive me for this partiality were I to justify it as the spirit of 'Christian charity' and if I were moved by my own goodness, like those good Samaritans discreetly getting their orgasms by rounding up their Sunday victim, media mystics bandaging their lepers in front of the television cameras, or the lascivious confessor firmly massaging a female sinner's soul. My case is outrageous only because I maintain that prostitution is not invariably an evil or a misfortune, nor is it the sickness of society as claimed.

In our tribal system the taboos on language are more inviolable than those on behaviour. No one actually casts a stone at the man who has recourse to the services of a whore, provided that he doesn't brag about it.

Such injustice isn't merely permissible but obligatory. If I consider prostitution a taint, it isn't so much because of its existence, but rather that the subject is treated so hypocritically. Prostitution has never been a problem to civilizations which were not ashamed of it and in which it had an honourable status.

In some circles it's customary to show oneself to be 'broadminded' on the subject, since 'men need it'. Maybe one should ask oneself whether some women too might not have a psychological and physical 'need' for prostitution. Such a question is strictly taboo. To ask it is considered more of an insult to female dignity than to assume that women only prostitute themselves strictly for the money.

Morality, the law, and public opinion are equally reluctant to admit that women may prostitute themselves *because they like doing so*. When I was rash enough to declare that the day might come (and sooner than we imagine) when some of my contemporaries might prostitute themselves *for pleasure*, I received the most frenziedly insulting letters in my post-bag. This response confirmed that the subject is among those which must not be discussed at any price.

I have, however, known stunningly beautiful and intelligent young women tremble at the thought of failing the examination set for them by Madame Claude (or some such classy procuress), displaying the same apprehension an actor feels before an audition.

Better still: I know (and am not the only one to know them!) several aspiring starlets who have deliberately abandoned theatrical careers in order to work full time as call-girls. (The reverse is also true, as every one is aware, and certain famous actresses have not been ashamed to admit it.)

All for the money? Up to a point, yes, but not for money *alone*. For an actor too, money talks, yet it isn't enough in itself. The pleasure of acting and that of feeling oneself to be in control, onstage, playing a part, are all worth more than the glamour. Not to mention the pleasure in itself . . .

Are Madame Claude's 'young ladies' the exceptions in the world of prostitution? They certainly represent a kind of élite, but the mentality of their less privileged sisters isn't always markedly different from that I have just described. Would one claim that the thousands of prostitutes who in June 1976 barricaded themselves inside churches in towns throughout France took such direct action purely out of stubbornness or because their pimps made them do so? Did they write to Valéry Giscard d'Estaing asking him to deliver them from their 'slavery'? Not likely! With great panache and an eloquence worthy of their national literary heritage they demanded the legal right to practise their chosen profession freely and safely. A profession they *liked* more than any other. And they called upon their president elect to act 'as president of the prostitutes and not just as president of the French in general'.

A fine civic address, which will, I hope, find a place in school textbooks of the future! It seems to me that these heroines are quite as commendable as those sanctified by a society that honours political sadism.

The French government responded to this brilliant challenge by setting packs of its police dogs on to the protesters. It looks as if mere men didn't feel up to the task of bringing whores to heel. They had to call up beasts.

It was also evident that the clergy of the occupied churches refrained from taking any action against the prostitutes camping in front of the altars. I am not qualified to expound upon the ancient relationship between prostitution and religion. I shall confine myself to suggesting that under the circumstances the prudence shown by the Church's representatives was in all likelihood the result of an age-old opportunism. Trusting in this ecclesiastical shrewdness, I can only conclude that prostitution is trendier now than ever. And although I know that I'll offend many of my friends (and supply welcome ammunition to my enemies), I feel pleased about that.

Why do my friends get indignant about my position on prostitution? For reasons I respect but reject. They explain such reasons to me thus: the philosophy of complete and free love, of intelligent, generous and disinterested love which I uphold is incompatible with the very concept of prostitution, since the latter is based on insincerity, pretence and greed. (Personally, I prefer to talk of diversity of benefits. See 'Payment in Kind' in *My Emmanuelle, their Pope and my Eros*, 1974).

Logically speaking, they are right. But I am not

always satisfied with abstraction. The love I pray for does not yet exist. What is worse, it never could exist *for everybody*. Many people would always remain absolutely incapable of putting it into practice; many others wouldn't have the physical or social good luck to share in it. For all these deprived people a prostitute's embrace is better than none at all.

But at least times are changing, and not only because priests can recall the words of Jesus to Mary Magdalene. A newspaper like *Le Monde* is not, perhaps, the recognized mouthpiece of bourgeois conformity, yet no one would imagine it issuing any statement sympathetic in principle towards prostitution. So I was quite astounded (as were, I suspect, the majority of its readers) when on 6 June 1975, I read on the front page – signed by one of its political commentators, Bertrand Fessard de Foucault – the following comments, entitled *The Greatest Misery*, which I'd happily have written myself:

'Heart and soul are one body, greedy to feel, to grasp and be grasped (. . .) To condemn or cheat (. . .) is just one further contemptible action by a society that has no room for more. (. . .) I know that people can literally die of lack of friendship, of not being loved and treated like normal flesh and blood beings. So I wonder whether these women – today in Lyons, but yesterday and tomorrow in other places – aren't right to claim some consideration and security in the work society makes them do, until the time we invent alternative family or communal structures or unless we deploy more happiness, freedom and courage in our quest for others and for ourselves.'

On reading that, it was as if I'd read something I'd written myself: an odd experience, particularly when prompted by a political journalist whose articles had previously never affected me so emotionally or personally! But I had to admit that I had misjudged him in the past (or that minds really do develop), for he continued:

'Our so-called liberal society makes schizoid beings of us all. For and against others we demand a morality and rules that we ourselves often consider inapplicable when it comes to our own misery or happiness. (. . .) I think the Lyons prostitutes, whose profession it is to look us straight in the eye, are crying out for far more than their personal interests. (. . .) The well-off can ignore them or mock. The deprived, even though on other occasions they might, because of upbringing or conformity, turn away, should – yes, should – recognize that this is their fight too. I think it a far more moral and sincere one than many others.'

Well, I'm going to be able to retire, because reinforcements are here! I'll refer any of my friends who bore me with their fine scruples to this decent and honest man. And even if I baffle them one last time, I find myself in cheerful agreement with that other contributor to *Le Monde* (whose wisdom and humour are well-known and appreciated), Professor Robert Escarpit.

In his short column 'From day to day', dated 7 June 1975, after recalling that 'in Mexico not so long ago, they were given the attractive nickname of *mariposas*, meaning butterflies', this moralist wishes that the law would make one requirement of prostitutes: that they should contribute towards making the environment better rather than worse. 'A pretty girl in the street is a pleasant sight, whatever she is doing,' he concludes. 'It should be the business of the Minister for the Quality of Life: if he understands his job properly, he himself is basically a "good-time man".'

When good-time girls stop seeming different from ourselves, it will be a good sign: it will mean that we ourselves will have gained what we most lack today, a zest for life and the good times. Then perhaps they too, like myself, will be able to relax.

A world without clitoris

Maureen no longer has a clitoris. She agreed with her lover to have it amputated. In order to please the man she loves, she has agreed never again to have an orgasm.

Throughout the world, of course, many women sacrifice their own pleasure for someone else, be that someone male or female. Many men, too. Usually though, they don't push such abnegation to the point of undergoing physical mutilation. At least that's what I thought until I met Maureen. From now on I won't be quite so sure.

Maureen is Irish. She lives in Singapore. To the best of my knowledge clitoridectomy is not the usual custom either in Ireland or south-east Asia . . .

'That's true,' she agreed. 'But I met my lover in Syria. There it can be done.'

'Or *has* to be done?' I tried to ascertain.

I didn't really understand whether Maureen was referring to a national tradition or expressing a personal conviction when she replied:

'It's a good thing to have it done.'

I persisted:

'What happened in your case? Did your lover insist on it?'

'He didn't insist. He just told me that he'd be glad if I didn't have a clitoris any more.'

'Was that so as to observe social rituals or ancient morality? Or out of crazy conformity?'

'Definitely not. He's very independent, cosmopolitan in his ideas and education, and not at all puritanical I assure you. He's the most sensual man I've ever known:

during the seven years I've been with him, he's gone on making love to me several times a day.'

'And he derives even more satisfaction from your no longer having a clitoris?'

'That's quite normal.'

'It's absurd. Quite simply, he was scared you might be unfaithful. By making you frigid he took the precaution of a jealous man, that's all.'

'You really don't know him at all: he's the very opposite of jealous. He makes me sleep with other men.'

'Prostitutes you?'

'No, he offers me only to his friends. Not for money.'

'Did he lend you, as it were, before he made you have your clitoridectomy?'

'Yes, he always has done, ever since our relationship began.'

'After asking your consent?'

'Of course.'

'Do you like him lending you or does it annoy you?'

'I'm happy he's proud of me.'

'And does he appreciate the pleasure you give his friends?'

'Very much. He's happy that I give them good orgasms.'

'As long as you don't come yourself!'

'A climax isn't important to me.'

'When you still had a clitoris, didn't you come?'

'Yes.'

'Every time you made love?'

'Yes. And very deeply.'

'Were you ashamed?'

'Ashamed? No. Why?'

'Because you wanted to give it up.'

'It wasn't my idea. My lover explained to me that he'd come even more if he could fuck me without my coming.'

'His friends too.'

'Maybe. But I was only thinking about him. I love only him.'

'And you believed what he told you, that a woman who didn't come would give a man a better orgasm than a woman who did come?'

'Certainly. I still think that's true.'

'I just have to admit that I can't make head or tail of what you're saying! As to its being true, that's just a joke surely!'

'I don't agree. If I were a man I wouldn't want my wife to come.'

'That's crazy! Can you tell me why not?'

'While coming she would stop belonging to me.'

'Well, for once I agree! And still on that subject, I don't suppose you can masturbate any more now?'

'No. Whenever I try, it hurts.'

'Some women never like playing with the clitoris. Perhaps you were one of them?'

'Not at all.'

'Did you masturbate, before?'

'The whole time.'

'Women who don't get much sensation from the clitoris have other means of reaching orgasm: via their vaginas, breasts, buttocks, mouths. There's plenty of choice!'

'Not for those who've had clitoridectomies.'

'Are you saying that they can no longer have orgasms any other way?'

'Right.'

'Because of the psychic trauma they've undergone?'

'Don't look for such clever explanations. They no longer *want* to come, it's as simple as that. And quite natural.'

' "Normal," and "natural" seem to be your favourite

words. What you consider natural and normal shocks *me*.'

'People are always scared of what they don't know.'

'Now that you, who enjoy using your own body, know what a body without a clitoris is like, do you have any regrets?'

'I sometimes remember occasions when I had orgasms and regret no longer being able to experience the sensation. But there are plenty of other things to interest me.'

'Your lover's pleasure, for instance?'

'Yours too . . .'

And it's quite true, she was caressing me marvellously expertly. Yet I'd have liked her to have an orgasm with me. I carried on questioning her, rather reluctantly:

'Your lover wouldn't like it if he knew what you were doing to me!'

'He does know. He doesn't mind.'

'In other words, he grudges you only the sensations in your clitoris. He couldn't care less about the rest of your inclinations.'

'It's not that he couldn't care less: he encourages them. I've already told you he likes me to make people come.'

'I can't quite make up my mind which of you scares me more: he with his sadism or you with your submissiveness.'

'Why do you love me, then?'

'Because you're beautiful. But I'm wrong.'

'Take advantage of my body and stop lecturing me.'

'Taking advantage of stupidity embarrasses me. Weren't you ever intelligent?'

'I have an economics degree.'

'Do you know any other women like yourself?'

'In my lover's country lots of women no longer have

clitorises. But they're not like me because no one has asked them their opinion.'

'Do do you pity them?'

'Pity them for what? Right now I'm not interested in their problems.'

'If you were to have a daughter, wouldn't you at least be interested in hers? Would you let her cut off her clitoris?'

'It's already been done. I have a daughter by my lover. And he's just had her clitoris cut.'

'What! . . . And you agreed?'

'I didn't need to give my consent.'

'And what about her, did she give hers?'

'She didn't need to either.'

'You're a monster and so is your lover! I could weep for your little daughter, not for you.'

'To qualify as monsters, all that's required is to disagree with you! And I thought you were liberal, tolerant, unconventional!'

'Where other people or myself are concerned I don't confuse freedom with the right to do wrong. I hate everything which deprives men and women of pleasure, hope, dignity and happiness. I fight against those who like to humiliate, dominate and cause suffering. And I'm equally opposed to people who like being humiliated and dominated and enjoy suffering.'

'You're wasting your time! Don't you read the newspapers?'

'Some of them, fortunately, do say much the same things as I.'

'To no more avail!'

Maureen, smiling, went and fetched a recent newspaper article she had cut out. It stated that the President of the international *Terre des Hommes* society, Edmond Kauseal had in April 1977 written an open letter from Geneva to the Secretary General of the United Nations, urging him to undertake 'a far-reaching campaign against the sexual mutilations suffered by millions of adolescent girls in numerous countries'.

His letter described in nightmarish detail these painful and bloody practices which he called 'the worst of rapes': clitoridectomy, excision of the labia minora, cutting of the labia majora without any anaesthetic and stitching of the vagina – later to be torn open by the husbands.

'Such torments,' the author goes on, 'sometimes result in the deaths of these children.' Those who survive pernicious anaemia, infections of the urethra, bladder and womb, abscesses on the vulva, perineal inflammation, gangrene, septicaemia and the tetanus these "operations" cause, carried out as they are by elderly women using dirty stones, bones or decaying shells, amid frenzied singing and dancing, generally become frigid for ever. Nowhere in the world is there any surgical means of making their bodies whole again or of restoring the erogenous sensation of which they have been deprived. The damage is irreversible. Their misery is irremediable.

In which unknown countries then, are these horrors being perpetrated? In at least thirty countries, quite openly and with the blessing of the authorities: notably in Saudi-Arabia, Syria, Jordan, the Yemen, Somalia, Kenya, the Sudan (the only country, according to the article, whose government is trying to discourage such customs), Libya, Zaire, Chad, the Ivory Coast – not counting all the other places in the world where male advocates of slavery have no difficulty finding doctors willing to cripple victims (voluntary or otherwise) like Maureen.

She was laughing.

'Poor M. Kauseal!' she said mockingly. 'There's no chance of anyone listening to his tirades! The economic and social council of the United Nations has tried at least once before (on 10 July 1958, as I recall: you see, I know all the facts!) to get the World Health Organization to ban these customs. That organization very wisely answered on 29 May 1959 that "the operations complained of were the result of social and cultural beliefs whose study is not within our competence".'

'What bastards!' I exclaimed.

'Anyhow, Emmanuelle,' said Maureen bluntly, 'what authority have *you* got to find fault with differences in cultures? Haven't people unlike yourself the right to prefer their customs to yours? Are you going to forbid them rituals that meet their particular needs, religions, fantasies and habits?'

'You ought to bear in mind that no religion ordains these mutilations.'

'True believers anticipate orders. I don't need to believe that a god is right in order to submit to him. It's enough for me to know he exists. My lover is this god.'

'And what faith consoles those women whose agreement isn't even asked?'

'Are sceptical women freer than I? Maybe they keep their clitorises physically, but have they the right to use them as they please, any more than having them cut off? At least *I* have the private satisfaction of having followed the logic of my faith to the very end.'

'For what promised paradise?'

'For love of my lover.'

'Real love is an art not a possession. Loving takes imagination, means becoming the lover's clitoris and enjoying what makes her come.'

'Right, well that's exactly what *I* do! I become my lover's sex and enjoy what makes him come.'

'It's true that *you* do, you're capable of love. But not of loving men: you said earlier that you only knew how to love gods. Your love is a sincere but inhuman passion. You love as if carrying out a religious sacrifice.

There, now I realize why I can't understand you: it's because you are religious. But you weren't born a believer, faith was forced upon you. Your clitoridectomy was the last sacrament given you by the prompting of an implacable conscience. And not by chance either: there is no more anti-religious organ in the world than the clitoris.'

'I was never taught that at school,' Maureen joked.

'You've been had!'

IV. The Breasts of Eros

Lara, or the shared look

I don't know whether, between the time of writing this and its publication, the public will have had the chance to see *Maladolescenza* or whether the custodians of public morals will have seen fit to ban it.

Thanks to Franco Cancellieri, who is distributing it in Italy, I went to a private screening of this film. But I won't be discussing it here in terms of good or bad, because that night my thoughts were preoccupied with other things than a subjective criticism of the fiction I was shown.

I'd known for some time that one of the stars of Pier Giuseppe Murgia's film was a girl of fourteen called Lara Wendel. Photographs of her which an Italian magazine, *Playmen*, had published in February 1977 had really intrigued me. Of course in this magazine the presence of a beautiful naked body, even that of so young a girl, was nothing unusual. Why had I been so amazed, then?

At first I thought it was the tenderness in her face, its latent humour, its self-assurance . . . But it wasn't that, it was really Lara Wendel's nakedness, and her nakedness alone, which aroused my interest.

Had I been struck by her age? Compared to her, though, her partner in the film, Eva Ionesco, who was also nude and very young, left me quite cold – while Lara's own image affected me more the longer I looked at it, affected me as if we were friends.

A friend isn't simply someone whose company I'm glad to have: a friend is someone who teaches me something. Lara naked didn't only appeal to my sensibility, sensuality and taste, she appealed to my intelligence. She communicated to me discernment and wisdom. And she was inviting me to share a sort of courage with her.

Naturally all nudity, even today, is courageous. Yet it wasn't so much her own strength of character which her nudity made me ponder, as the cowardice of those watching her.

Not that of *everyone* watching, of course! But there were quite a few there who only dared look askance at her or who ogled her slyly, ashamed of their thoughts and desires, while whispering and even insulting her out loud – or (which wasn't much better) making excuses for her nakedness.

If cowardice debases and falsifies and makes everything seem sad, that is because it first manifests itself in our way of looking. Nothing scares us so much as sight.

Evil seems to hide everywhere, we think, even behind fine appearances, and this because we ourselves spend most of our time hiding our desires from others. We are evilminded, ugly, unhappy and solitary because we live with our heads in the sand.

Teaching us to look with our eyes open wide; teaching us to look boldly, and calmly, without insincerity or shiftiness; teaching us to look *properly*: that, as I finally understood, was what Lara was able to do. But I couldn't have understood without actually meeting her in the projection room.

She too had been invited, along with her mother, her younger brother, and a man who might have been her father. The behaviour of their group helped me see more clearly that it was precisely that which I ought to do.

Throughout the film I only looked at the screen in order to know what they themselves were looking at and how they did so. But I learned something from the way Lara was watching. She it was who showed me how one should gaze on naked limbs, on budding breasts and pubis, on a smile which promises sex, on lips caressing organs, on a woman giving herself and a man losing himself, on amorous and carnal joys that outmanoeuvre time, but also on the primitive repetition of unhappiness, on the injustice of desertion, on irrational jealousy, on the absurdity of tragedy, on the dreadful paradox of wanting to die, and on the derision of the lover who kills.

If I was able to see things this way – which might otherwise not have affected me so much – it was simply because Lara, seated quite near me, knew how to look, and more important, knew how to look at *herself*.

While doing so she was not (I felt) indulging herself in narcissism, nor displaying self-complacency: she was sincerely seeking to progress.

She was honestly trying to find out more, the better to understand that unknown adolescent on the screen who was laughing and enjoying herself just like she did, who hoped and suffered just like herself. And in order to do this, she was gazing with a look of affection, a tender look, at this screen double who was herself.

Looking at ourselves in mirrors or photographs doesn't often make us happy. This is because we nearly always see ourselves as others see us. And we know quite well that others rarely look on us kindly.

The distress we feel on thus discovering the peculiarity of our own faces or learning that our bodies are travesties, is therefore, in the end, the same thing we feel when we look at others. And the perpetual carousel of subterfuges, hypocrisy and mutual malice goes round and round for ever . . .

This girl with the radiant expression (and here I had an almost physical sensation of her absolute conviction) did not consider herself to be alone. She credited those surrounding her in the darkness with judgment and taste. She thought them, in these respects, her equals.

Was it out of childish ignorance and generous

candour? No, for I saw that young though she was, she knew what the world and life were about, and what was at stake.

Lara was not content to think us solely capable of admiring her beauty: she wanted us also to experience what she was feeling.

She wanted our eyes and hers to see together. She wanted them to see the same things and see them as clearly.

If she thought such participation feasible, it was because she wanted to be happy – and she knew that no happiness is possible without the shared look.

When the film was over, many of the audience came up to her. They did not look at her like casual crowds gaping at a star, but as if they could have embraced her.

I was among them and admired her in silence for some little time. Then I attempted to speak to her. But the few childish words of German which came to my mind were like smiles and songs. They came from so far away, with their harsh sweetness – from my young girl's mouth; their whispers reminding me of the time when my youth and beauty resembled her own – when I was like her . . .

I couldn't have actually said any of this. Instead I fumbled awkwardly for 'grown-up' words, abstract and over-refined, which, had I uttered them, would not have expressed what I wanted to say to Lara.

She guessed as much and smiled at me – less, I think, from sympathy for my embarrassment than from the premonition that one day she too might be tongue-tied and distanced from someone she liked. She came closer, took one of my hands in hers and seemed to be waiting . . . For what? For me to rejoin her across the truant years, as the schoolgirl I once was – or because she didn't know either?

Then this briefly-encountered double returned to her own time, to a world far from my own, leaving me alone amid people my own age.

Already now that memory is obscured. Did I ever really experience that meeting? Did I really see Lara looking at herself in the darkness, or did I by closing my eyes conjure up the vision my soul required?

Everything I desire exists: here or far away; at present in her, but in others to come. All that my childish sensuality lusted after, all that my womanly senses still long to know, someone somewhere will fulfil.

And that someone can be with me if I know how to love him or her.

But can I call that a certainty? Or are dreams replacing reality?

Lara's look, living in real life, always gives me the same answer. Reality, it teaches me, doesn't depend on me, but is dependent on my desires.

Everything, I believe, is possible, provided I am not alone in thinking so.

Lara isn't a mythical hallucination, she stands for nakedness and the look.

Nakedness and looking: two freedoms made socially inaccessible to us although we cannot enjoy them alone.

Nakedness and looking: intelligence only the memory is still capable of, whose future beauty we already half imagine.

Is it really the future? Or will body and consciousness indefinitely remain for us an imaginary prospect?

Tell us Lara! Come back and tell us in a language everyone can understand: do freedom, intelligence and humanity have a chance on this earth, or must we, dressed-up monkeys that we are, be content for ever only to dream?

Bianca, or the nocturnal side

I amazed my friend Bianca. I told her: 'You are an artist'. She didn't even know! For years she's been writing stories which the various magazines she has approached have published without quibbling, almost on receipt. She never sends them out with any comment or request. The alacrity of her editors might have made her smell a rat. But no, she still doesn't even realize she is producing works of art . . .

Of course writing alone doesn't make one an artist. The art must be inside a man before being in his work. An artist is someone who desires, invents, expresses. And above all someone who strives to bring *perfection* to what he does, never relaxing such efforts. Naturally the species is a rare one!

The pains taken, the hours spent, insomnia, attention to detail, the will to be precise, to refine and embellish, to review and re-create, the search for the striking image and the humblest of words, the feel for sound and the love of rhythm – all these and many other splendid torments, experienced obsessively, distinguish the true artist from the dilettante, the poseur and the trifler. The latter are quickly tired and easily pleased; they smugly convince themselves that their rough drafts are 'quite good as they are', indeed 'not at all bad', and that anyhow there's nothing to add or delete, nothing to improve.

The artist, however, is pledged to an inveterate dissatisfaction. The pursuit of images which constantly elude the expression is the only really serious occupation in life. This passion taxes but never exhausts him.

Everything Bianca writes is the product of this mania for perfection. To me who reads it, the result is perfect. Yet my attractive friend refuses to think of herself as an artist. Is this out of timidity, discretion or scepticism? Is it because she doesn't work on a large scale, doesn't resort to the kind of lyrical effusions that are taken to be 'literary', or because she doesn't rehash those moralizing abstractions which make the reputations of lesser mortals? From time to time Bianca simply sets down a low key and sometimes not immediately striking episode about someone quite ordinary. How is it then that these accounts fire my imagination, nudge my intelligence and stick in my memory? Why does reading her stories give me so much pleasure and why do I so admire their author? Since it isn't the unusual or excessive behaviour of their protagonists which moves me, it must be the particular manner of narration.

Of course the object on which the artist's vision is concentrated is not necessarily what interests us most. A painter may reproduce apples or nudes; a novelist may be describing love or war: what makes them into someone who fulfils our secret desires is the way they make us see what we would not otherwise have seen; to feel what we wouldn't have felt so keenly; to want what we wouldn't have known how to want. Also, above all, the artist offers *us* the unexpected opportunity of inhabiting his imagination.

Philosophers, priests, politicians, scientists all presume to think for us and to act on our behalf. Our participation in their tasks isn't really required, unless it takes the form of deference and acceptance. Our conscience and presence is to them more often an annoyance than a necessity.

As for the artist, he cannot do without us. He may seem to be isolating himself, to prefer isolation to ourselves, but this is a mood, an affectation. If we were to take him at his word and leave him communing with Nature, would he dedicate his creation to her? And what would she make of it?

Nature, whatever a lazy tradition may claim, doesn't give the poet such pleasure. He finds her regrettably botched, ill-made, and in a word, imperfect. Her author really put her together any old how! Any artist worthy of the name would have retouched and redesigned her meticulously, with far more love and skill. Which is exactly what the creative man sets out to do, morning till night: to remake the created world.

He doesn't always undertake this knowingly, and doesn't think about it deliberately. Often he wants to take reality as model and reproduce things as he sees them, only dealing with what he knows. Yet he cannot look at anything without that thing changing before his eyes and becoming something else. And he never quite knows in advance what he will end up understanding – and ultimately making us understand: that rarely boils down to what we already knew.

When she sits down at her desk Bianca may well believe (and promise us too) that she only intends to take us for a Sunday trip from Vicenza to Ferrara with herself and her lover. But she has scarcely written two sentences before the autostrada lined with parapets and guard-rails, suddenly becomes another world.

Did the incident related decide the future of the characters? Or was it Bianca's typewriter? Certainly the destiny of the lovers wouldn't have followed the same course had they journeyed only into actuality. The sterility of their relationship would not have seemed so clear to them and we ourselves would probably never have recognized it: the truth would not have had so palpable an existence had not the writer's imagination supremely *created* a crisis and – consciously or unconsciously – *desired* one.

Indeed the artist, even more than he is an inventor, is a militant fighter for desire. The happiness of those for whom living is enough, and who like being what they have been, having what they have had, doing what they have done, is incomprehensible to him and fills him with horror. The artist never finds any possession which gratifies him, never considers any work or action completed, never finds a place which seems his own.

It isn't his acquired experience which makes him an artist but the further experiences he desires. In his eyes, everything he has already done is worthless, only serving to define what must not be repeated. The friends he has had, the loves he has known, the countries he has visited, have only made him certain of one thing: he can and must discover something further. Real inventors have no memory. Real creators have no country.

From paradise lost to imaginary paradise, these exiles without nostalgia recognize no equals, acknowledge no inheritance. To them every near is far, just as every landscape is unfamiliar. It is their sycophants who classify them and talk of 'schools' and 'works', because people without imagination need to prey on others in order to feel alive themselves. The genuine artist usually only feels disaffection, disgust and rejection towards the work he has accomplished and those with whom he has worked. He only feels at home among ideas he has not yet had; assumes responsibility only for acts he has not yet dared perform: and the sole ambition with which he is not disillusioned is that of expressing the inexpressible.

So the disturbing relationships linking art and desire are not essentially different from those which subordinate love to dream. Art and love are just around the corner or else they would only be happy memories. Art and love are a future side of ourselves which is still only a nocturnal side.

But the future and the night are fiction. A work of art without fiction would thus be as hypocritical as a love without hallucinations. The lucidity love sometimes retains isn't always what makes us most in love: for the same irrational reasons we do not ask art to remind us of our limitations. The function of art, like that of love, is to divert us.

The road by which the lovers who set out from Vicenza find themselves back at Ferrara, strangers, thus takes *us* much further than Bianca foresaw. However, I surprised my friend even more than I had by calling her an artist, when I told her she was erotic . . .

'I erotic? I never write a line about sex. I am not even sure my characters sleep together! Anyway, they never say a word about it. I'm even more reticent than they.'

Quite, it's not necessary. To be erotic, one doesn't need to undress the characters: Bianca confines herself to describing empty bathrooms.

Besides, how can we doubt that all art is in itself erotic? Eroticism is the expression of a desire for love which only the imaginative remodelling of chance and the challenge to necessity can satisfy.

Art and love alike are unnatural attempts to give to men more than they need and to sex more than it's accustomed to having. To make love other than as Nature inspires and Society dictates is to make a work of art. To write, paint, construct, or sing is already to make love.

Nature and Society offer us all we need, yet art persists in desiring and love goes on dreaming. Nature and Society impress and dominate: art and love express and question. Nature has given us a tongue and Society a language, but only art and love make us want to speak. To speak to each other.

That's why Bianca, you are erotic without wanting to be, for art is love without knowing it. You are so because the stories you invent speak of, for and to others. And eroticism is sex speaking.

Assumptions that sing

To how many of my contemporaries does art mean anything other than conformity, pessimism, hypnosis, habit and boredom?

Do they visit an art gallery to assimilate new forms and gain courage to live to the full?

Do they read a book in order to know characters more attractive, more intelligent, and more likeable than themselves?

Do they go to the theatre to explore parallel worlds?

Do they listen to a song in order to learn how to dream outrageous dreams?

Do they go to all this trouble just to brush up on their culture before producing it at the dinner-table?

No. The majority only indulge in such status games from self-denial, melancholy or a sense of duty.

But do the creators of image, sound and written fiction always offer them the chance of escaping from this dehumanizing routine?

Can one reproach the public for its apathy when the painter persists in copying the same messy daubs? When the novelist spews up the same jeremiad for the hundredth time? When the composer warbles any old phrase, the same refrains which made our parents complain or yawn – or (and this is no more entertaining) hammers out the same tired rock riffs which jerked the young into action last year or the year before?

Contrary to what these bunglers readily claim, so as to excuse their laziness, the emptiness of the spectacle isn't the spectator's fault. The artist's function is not to give the public what it asks for, since the public never asks for anything: it secretly hopes, hopes for the *new*. The artist who force-feeds it with hoary clichés insults this hidden expectation. He is stealing a promised joy from his public. His own lack of imagination or invention do not, as far as the public is concerned, add up to extenuating circumstances.

It is scandalous that the cowardice of the art-world allows the artist to go unpunished. I demand a merciless popular justice for the defamatory artist! Its first condition would be to oblige the creator to create. He will be forbidden to be repetitious or banal on pain of public deprivation of speech and gesture. The crime of banality would rate a sentence of ten years' silence. Acceptance of fate to be punished by perpetual ridicule.

What exactly do I mean here by 'acceptance of fate'? As you may already have guessed, I'm thinking of a certain idea (and practice) of love which for four or five hundred years at least has been dinning into our ears. It's not any old love, of course, but 'love' in inverted commas which our civilization persists in regarding as a problem and fearfully refuses to accept as potential innovation and pleasure.

It is common knowledge that even today, with a few rare exceptions, all alleged works of fiction are merely dismal rehashes of romantic tricks, sickly illusions, silly hopes and illiterate dreams. A stage play or film has only a slim chance of production or screening (except by those of remarkable insight and intuition) if they don't show that 'there's no such thing as happy love'. To be successful, the love-makes-art brigade think everything must be presented in terms of tragedy or farce: nothing but aggressive and vociferous cuckolds or hapless and happy ones.

The songwriting scene scarcely bears thinking about – those songs in which love invariably calls for rain and tears. 'Falling' in love is, judging by the lachrymose voices of our singers, a foolish blunder, a mug's game exploited sooner or later by the bastard or slut over whom one weeps none the less ... What a dull concoction! Music only acknowledges the stupid or deceitful lovers: the idea of happy and intelligent lovers is usually only touched upon in terms of a joke.

Yet such lovers do exist. Why not film them more, or sing more often of their pleasures? Is it through fear of censorship? No, I don't harbour any resentment against writers, film-makers and musicians: they're all too capable of surviving that. What they are not so good at doing, on the other hand, is escaping from the tradition of the lament. Every one of them more or less secretly subscribes to Alfred de Musset's famous credo, according to which 'the most beautiful songs are the most despairing'... The sadness, boredom and the rancid flavour of their works in general, together with the clichés with which many of these lugubrious-looking buffoons stupefy us and the mutual plagiarism to which they are given, are the logical consequences of this cynical aesthetic principle.

But art criticism isn't my job. My curious chosen profession involves the upheaval of amatory customs. In order to render obsolete the sentiments and morals which make us suffer irrationally, I imagine a love which will help us solve our problems instead of setting us insoluble ones ... And I'd like others to take up this vocation with me.

The love I dream of doesn't assume that desire is a failing or pleasure a sin. Its only hypothesis is that our freedom depends on others. Nor does it acknowledge that loving confers upon the lover a proprietary right over the beloved.

The love I dream of is based on certain assumptions, but these seem to me to offer more possibilities to the imagination and for happiness than our old principles did.

The first of these assumptions is that I can enjoy my lover's pleasure even if the lover is gaining that pleasure from another. Jealousy thus disappears at once from my universe.

Second assumption: my love is neither unique nor exclusive. Several lovers seem to me preferable to one. And I don't ask them to love only me, nor do I expect them to love me all of the time: Dr Hirsch's 'half a loaf' (in John Schlesinger's *Sunday, Bloody Sunday*) is enough to keep me happy too. Because of this, my world is also devoid of the deception of monosexuality and monogamy (I use 'deception' advisedly, for the institutions which consecrate such mentality and make such behaviour compulsory are founded on hypocrisy and their rules need breaking).

Third assumption: I do not hold back when I open my arms. Love is not a limit, or a barrier which I close against others and myself: it's a door I am opening for them and myself into a world that interests us, a world as rich and unknown as that of a savage tribe upon an unexplored island. To me love is not security, it is freedom. If I love, I have to be able to do without the one I love, from love of him – or to deprive him of me. I must be able to leave him be, to let him alone, to let him leave. I must be able to lose him. Loving one another is also knowing how to part. Also knowing how to forget.

I have tried to write about this sort of love in my books. I now try to discuss it still more clearly using other means. But I'd like others who share my beliefs to join with me in making this possible future *artistically* understood: I say artistically because only art can truly foresee our future tastes. Politics, religion and even science have proved their derisory inadequacy in this field: we take a sly (and justifiable) pleasure in always liking the opposite of whatever they have in store.

So I'd like those artists who like me dream of a love which will be a reason for living, to stop extolling death and to try celebrating life. I'd like them to cease talking of love tearfully and to learn to sing of love laughingly. I'd like their images and music to announce this possible love as if it were to be a sudden transformation of thought and emotion upon our planet, as if it were to be the approaching emergence of a new and amazing potential in our unpredictable species.

In a word, I'd like love stories and love songs, photographs and films about love, to inspire optimism – for it does exist, and not all prophets and forecasters are necessarily doomwatchers. It would be paradoxical if the artists, those dwellers in dreamland, were to prove gloomier prophets than the social planners who predict catastrophe.

Will I be reproached for asking the impossible of art? Of course not! The intuition the artist needs for looking into the future doesn't really require any skill in science fiction. And these days the freedoms the artist is brave enough to appropriate only very rarely cost him his own freedom or life. Earlier, I called down upon him the thunderbolts of an imaginary justice: I was only joking! Those who know me know quite well that repression isn't my line. Anyhow, it's not the courts which worry the artist most, but lack of success. Now in art success obeys various laws which I've already formulated elsewhere (*The Hypothesis of Eros*). To paraphrase them:

1. He who can only recreate what the public liked yesterday is not an artist. (Experience also teaches that he isn't necessarily a shrewd businessman either.)

2. He who foresees and expresses what the public will want to see or hear in a hundred years' time will be called (in a hundred years' time!) an unrecognized genius.

3. He who wants to be recognized during his lifetime merely as a genius must today guess and create what

the public will be able to like *tomorrow*. The fortunate artist is only one night ahead of his public.

But men's days and nights don't have the predictable regularity of cosmic revolutions. Man's spiritual and biological adventure upon earth is not subject to the inexorable determinism which governs the daily routine of the quanta flow. The ramshackle laws which decided their appearance continue to control their destiny. The laws are those of chance. And the only principle of which we can be sure is that of uncertainty.

The past and future history of humanity is essentially a game. The dice thrown by each of us during our lifetimes, does not abolish chance: it challenges it.

The artist is a master of this game. The work he creates is always a challenge, since it is a modification of Nature, a correction of chance. Yet the artist, like all men, is all the while free to gamble for better or worse.

When betting on the inevitable failure of love, the artist gambles for the worse. If he decides on the opposite, just for once, playing love triumphant – a love whose rules he himself would henceforth determine – love might really start winning, just as Nature sometimes begins to resemble the canvases of those who paint her.

We mustn't forget, after all, that artists are the inventors of a reality which is more real to us than the invisible structures of atoms and ecosystems, a reality the world would never have discovered unaided: I mean beauty.

A book or a film or a song which would portray a love without jealousy, fears or regrets – a triumphant, generous, joyful love – would be just as beautiful as a song of despair. Maybe it would be more useful. It would at any rate be less boring.

The inimitable act

Why do I mention art so often? My readers would no doubt prefer me to write about sex.

But what use is it if we just stop there, with what Nature has made of us? To me it seems more exciting to envisage what we might make of her. And I don't really see what we can make of Nature unless it's something else.

The refusal to resign ourselves to being what we are can certainly take other forms than artistic creation: for example, mystical evasion, political ambition, obsession with money or destructive violence, to mention only the most widespread. These attempts at altering destiny, however, have in common cynicism and a negativity which seem to me mistaken enough to satisfy those whom the natural absurdity of life depresses.

Patronizing astrologers, mythifiers and theologists usually make us even more nervous than we already are. As for political power, it rarely reassures either those wielding it or paying for it. Business, as the saying goes, never ends – without ending in tears. As for terrorism, its explicit belief in fighting evil with evil approximates so nearly to that of religious faith that it does no more than religion to find appropriate solutions.

So for as long as it has existed, neither the fear of God, nor political skill, nor financial acumen, nor widespread warfare have made us substantially happier or clearly less stupid. We must think about looking elsewhere.

Where? Only art remains. But which art?

Photography, song, dance, weaving?

From my own experience I recommend an apprenticeship in that intimately human art to which I can give no other name but eroticism, even if the ambiguity of the word sometimes gives rise to farcical misunderstandings.

Eroticism is, in my opinion (this is doubtless my hundredth definition of it, and probably not the last!) one form of the art of life, consisting of thwarting, through imagination and invention, the moralizing prosaic aspects of our sexual customs, and of replacing our off-the-peg amorous suits with tailor-made fantasies.

If sex is to become more advanced, however, wouldn't it be more in order for us to look to sexology, or to put it another way, to science rather than to art?

But is sexology as we know it today really a science?

When it limits itself to collecting and disseminating psychological, social and biological information which was previously unavailable or difficult to obtain, I'll listen to it with an open mind. Such instruction might help me know myself and others better. Unfortunately our contemporary sexologists are only too quick to give us advice and put pressure upon us when all we want from them are facts. Their alleged science thus hinges on morality. And since all morality is of its essence a mixture of religion, politics, and violence, even the most curious findings by sexologists don't in the end alter the restrictions our more familiar rulers have made us obey.

So the improvement (or rather the indefinite re-creation) of our sexual condition has more chance of realization when conceived as an art than when we embark upon it out of concern for mental and physical health, through piety or good citizenship, as an investment on trust or from revolutionary fervour.

A further question has to be asked here: what is art?

It seems to me that art is simply a free invention with pleasure in mind.

Free from what? Free in the first place of course, from the tastes and opinions of others. Free also from the natural attachments, mental patterns and social rites which ensure our position in a world of submission.

Yet we like these ties and customs and we don't free ourselves from them as willingly as all that! They identify us with the past, and reassure us against the terrifying unknown which the future represents for us. The illusion of security they give us is usually far more important than freedom. That is why art more readily inspires our distrust than our liking . . .

Well, we are right to fear the worst! For art urges us to do no less than cast off our last uniforms, get rid of our automatic responses, and do without our ultimate secrets and fidelities.

Indeed, being an artist, primarily, is wanting to be an individual. And also, not letting oneself be easily reassured.

'The artist is not the world's recorder but its rival,' said André Malraux just before his death. And the world has always understood this only too well: hence its hostility.

The only truthful ambition of art is to challenge the existing world so as to construct another more malleable world closer to man's liking. Some people have adjudged this intrusion of the will into creation blasphemous and immoderate: but on this count, isn't life itself more of a threat than anything else to the peace of God? If he had been logical, he would have made an inanimate world.

In any case, it would be futile to lament the fact that artistic ambition is never fully realized. The characteristic feature of art is not to set itself limits, and existence itself, after all, has no limits either.

What place has love in all this?

Precisely that which the artist agrees to give his art.

And the role of art in love is to challenge ideas and practices emanating from our basic instincts and which our societies dictate.

The creative mind tirelessly proposes disconcerting substitutes for such ideas and practices. All this at the expense of immortality, for much later other artistic minds will invent new images to replace in their turn the creations of today, which will have become outmoded.

But why give us so much suffering? Because our lives are played out only once and we must play at living in order not to let ourselves be played upon by life.

The innovation and infinite renewal which art is capable of bringing to love is the chance of a game without rules, where no move is ever repeated. The future henceforth takes on the savour of a promised party, which our inherited fears would deny us. And it offers us possibilities of new experiences from which we might emerge unscathed.

Winning in love, however, won't ever have the same meaning as succeeding in business. The erotic victory will always depend upon man's ability to prefer a more distant pleasure to an immediate experience. Well, there are no objects more distant than the men or women one loves.

Clearly this sort of consciousness assumes other dimensions and values than those of commercial arithmetic and domestic investment. Its dividends, though, are enough to increase infinitely the capital of desire: the only sort of which we need not be ashamed and which cannot ultimately embarrass us.

Art, in sum, is the product of a refusal of fate, which makes us choose the hazard of metamorphoses rather than the security of death. It is thus the least ridiculous and deceptive answer one can give to that question which would otherwise remain open: *What can man do?*

What the artistic option can prompt man and woman

to accomplish is analogous to the disturbing creativity of their act when making love without wanting a child. The order of things is naturally upset by this, as are the father-confessor, the soldier, the real estate agent, the dictator. *Giving pleasure* is neither sacred nor warlike, neither profitable nor docile: it isn't even *natural*.

But to please is profoundly *artistic* and the reason for this, more than anything else, shocks the silent majority and the supporters of the Establishment because it is inimitable!

An inhuman obligation to silence

'You do not understand what I am saying: that is your fault and your misfortune!' Mayakovsky was right to talk to his contemporaries so frankly. He was a poet. A nation that does not try to understand what her poets are telling her consigns herself to subjection. Men could be free: they submit because they like it.

There are two worlds within ours: a world of knowledge and a world of wilful ignorance. Freedom will never belong to the latter, for there is no freedom in silence and ignorance, just as there is no power without the word. Control of knowledge finally comes back to communication.

In our world, then, who knows how to speak?

Firstly, the politicians and priests. Next the scientists and the philosophers. Finally, the artists.

What do these privileged users of language say?

Politicians and clergy by definition talk the idiom of power. As for the experts and the scientists, they do not usually deal with the problems of power. Their jargon isolates them and deprives them of any direct influence over the masses, while this linguistic gap can only broaden the more science progresses. In this area, therefore, the security of the politicians is assured. Scientists seize power only in science fiction books!

Philosophers and pure ideologues are equally inoffensive. The reason for this is that since religions are past it, ideologies have come to adopt the language of science. In so doing they have become unable to make themselves accessible to the average man, unable to get through to him.

Only the artist remains as standard-bearer of communicable ideas. Not only is he free, should he wish, to speak a language everyone can understand but he also holds the power to get others talking it.

In fact people actually do things and behave according to the dictates of fashion. Yet fashion is no more than the residual form of discoveries originally voiced by the artist.

Before corrupting itself by imitation and descent to conformity, fashion always starts as subversion. It is its followers who do all they can to regiment it, vulgarize it and make it last. As for its creators, they are usually only concerned with causing controversy and always going for the shock effect.

Their fashions without any clearly discernible purpose answer a secret need which differentiates us from other mammals. This irrepressible and incalculable need I have previously characterized (in *The Hypothesis of Eros*) as leading us towards 'pleasure in losing'.

One simply needs to classify this mental and social impulse to understand at once why it is unacceptable in terms of power, when the cast-iron rule of all power is winning.

Art, however, isn't just pleasure in losing: still more obviously it's pleasure in speaking. This second characteristic is no less revolutionary than the first, since control of free speech is a vital element in power. Inherent in all free speech is the end of universal subjection.

The world would be silent if the poet did not have the ability to speak for all men. Men's silence would indeed be awesome if the poet's hope were not to announce the changing of words, the movement of things and the slow humanization of laws.

The poet's function, whatever form it may take, sooner or later boils down to saying No. It is the nature of power to stifle this No, whether by killing whoever shouts it (Neruda), by imprisoning them (Solzhenitzyn) or by defaming their controversial products (films by Bertolucci and Pasolini).

In the most obviously despotic countries (the USA, France), resorting to degrading classifications (such as 'X' films), to new taboos or outworn superstitions, to monetary controls, to religious mania or the ready militancy of neurotics – all effectively serves to divert and protect the politicians from their age-old fear, the fear of losing power.

People would know nothing of this, everyone would find ideological and moral progress impossible, the appointed propagandists would talk about the inevitable swing of the pendulum and Nature's revenge, the moralists would urge repentance and new gods would mushroom, if the real artists were not around to spill the beans.

Friendlier and more intelligible prophets than the scientists, these creators of images and signs threaten the future of politicians even more than they spoil their present. For power not only needs current knowledge, but depends above all upon accurate prediction.

The artist better than anyone is equipped to guess what men may understand or want, what they may wish to experience or be capable of loving and doing tomorrow.

In a word, the artist is, of all of us, the nearest to the truth.

Truth is not a collection of fixed data which some authority has reserved: it is the provisional result of questioning, and constant revision of knowledge. It changes from day to day in contact with further realities.

The truth of the universe of which man is a part cannot therefore be contained or immobilized by any law, whether that law sees itself as scientific, human or

Godgiven. That sad little 'sense of decency' is no more enlightened than the Holy Fathers or the Hare Krishna children. All the more reason why it should never be endorsed by a civil or penal Code or by moral rules, or even by a comprehensive science. Heisenberg died this year knowing that his successors would never see the most recently discovered particle 'epsilon' more clearly than he himself, no matter how expert they might become . . .

Truth, to sum up, does not reside in things. It is the ever-changing yet valuable product of our desires, sincerity and freedom.

Whenever a book enriches our desires, puts our sincerity to the test, and fights for our freedom, its courage gives us strength to forge forward ever further in search of our truth.

Since I quoted him at the start of this piece, maybe Mayakovsky should have a further opportunity to affirm this relationship between art and life. When he says that 'the realization of an end is only thinkable through the means of a poetic work', he is offering us the most definite hope we can imagine. In a time when the intellect would like us to doubt whether our existence has a purpose, poetic intuition is our only way of knowing that happiness is this purpose.

Authority senses this. Whenever it condemns a book, cuts or burns a film, pours scorn upon a work of art, it does so not because it cares about our intelligence and happiness, but in order to prevent a new truth being created (and in Greek, *poiesis* means creation). All truth, except that emanating from power itself, terrifies power. And all power when terrified adopts terror.

Power dreads eroticism not because it thinks it capable of enslaving bodies better than itself, but because eroticism is an art and all art frees the spirit.

All the same, authority is anxious whenever morality becomes freer, since every erotic act is a search for truth. Authority is damn right to be scared of men and women who practise honesty in love, who seek to become more imaginative in their sexual relationships, who consider that the old virtues of the couple, marriage, and the family need changing! Some day perhaps, these men and women will get the idea that the forces and political structures dominating them, can also be renovated.

The taste for truth and the use of freedom which eroticism involves is, according to the Vatican, a sign of 'grave disorders'. (In its documents on sexual ethics published on 15 January 1976, by the Committee for doctrinal matters, formerly the Holy Office of the Roman Curia, each of the condemnations pronounced is justified by the fact that the behaviour censured constitutes 'a grave disorder'. What is more, one reads therein that 'man sins mortally when he makes a choice, freely and knowingly, for whatever motive, whose object is that of grave disorder'. Order reigns in the Vatican while love is unknown there.) Yes, the Vatican really knows what's what!

Yet biology shows us that the progress of life is not expressed by any fixed order: it manifests itself, with each leap forward and through the increasing complexity of matter, via the creation of a higher order.

Eroticism is art, but biology too. The artist himself is a biologist in his way. Both deal simultaneously with mind, body and life. They know that mind and body undergo dangerous changes. And they try to change life by upsetting the moral order.

Thus it is normal for those who conserve that order to label the erotic artist abnormal. It is natural that the fear they have of hearing him disturb their world of silence misrepresents his work.

But love will always be in advance of the order of the day.

In order that time may stand still in their ordered world, rulers may well pronounce that speech is abnormal and love against nature: but as long as the artist, risking all, continues to make desire accessible to us, we shall know that nothing is against Nature.

Power and knowledge, or the eternity of the stake

The Law sends films to the stake.[1] Or, which is worse, movie producers, fearing magistrates, trim the completed work of directors they have lured with promises of absolute artistic control. Their tampering makes a nonsense of such work; their conformism vulgarizes it; their cowardice disfigures it; their cheap commercialism prostitutes it; their obsequious greed debases it – far more than the limited brutality of the state executioners would have dared do.

Innocence and hope die hard, so are we right in saying that this era is too grim to last? Can we safely predict that such incredible outrages can only be perpetrated by a reactionary rearguard? Or that the illiterate fanaticism of these mutilations, the idiocy of the cutting, the wilful triviality and pretentious perfidy of the dubbing, and these pointless persecutions are destined to end in the near future?

No, we cannot predict any such thing.

We are naïve – and our naïvety threatens our mental and physical stability – if we imagine that the ruling class will, as a result of polite requests, give up censorship, or the other forms of oppression it is currently employing against artistic expression. It has neither the

[1]*Note:* In January 1976 the Italian Court of Cassation decreed that all existing copies and even the negative of Bernardo Bertolucci's *Last Tango in Paris* should be burnt. *Salo, or the 120 Days of Sodom* (Pasolini) narrowly escaped the same fate. Dozens of other films are seized everywhere daily, banned and awaiting destruction, even in England where free speech is a tradition. In France now they are branded, as in the days of the monarchy, and impounded just like before the Revolution!

intention nor (even if it wished) the means. Its violence is not an improvization of circumstances. The subjection of art is the very condition of the exercise and survival of power.

No power is possible in our society without the monopoly of knowledge. Art, and erotic art in particular, offends Power not because it distracts or diverts citizens, but because it gives them information.

What is more, this art blithely assumes the right to disseminate its knowledge in its own way, without asking the State's permission.

And how these stateless ideas appeal to the public! From them the public derives a new zest for instruction. It feels the urge to think differently. It believes in the possibility of changing life.

Now all knowledge that reaches the people other than through authority threatens the existence of that authority itself. The interdependence between power and knowledge is so close that one cannot survive without the other.

Even in feudal society, the real supremacy was not in the hands of the secular lords but belonged to the Church, the exclusive dispenser and withholder of information and thus of hope. Her empire did not survive the emergence of a temporal science. For the bourgeois State, which has benefited from this transference of knowledge and maintains its appropriation through an inflexible educational hierarchy, sharing information would be just as fatal.

The war this State today wages against eroticism has no other objective than to prevent such a sharing process. The State does not act out of moralistic fervour, but from conservative instinct. It knows that its ideology is incompatible with the aim of eroticism. Society must choose one or the other.

The aim of eroticism is *all-inclusive* – in daily life as

in art. By contrast the bourgeois system, in the manner of the aristocratic and clerical regimes from which it stemmed, defines itself by a rigid code of functions by *exclusion*.

Within this system, public and private good and evil are in essence blurred but have clearly-defined limits. These demarcation lines however are no more 'natural' or just than national frontiers. They were not fixed as the result of an analysis of men's needs, or of their desire for happiness, but were chosen arbitrarily.

Yet these moral boundaries, like the frontiers between States can only be defended by the majority, which will act only if indoctrinated with a *faith* that continues to keep it governable. In other words it will be incurious, predictable, immutable and immobile.

To understand a culture of domination then, one must know its limits rather than studying its inner structures and myths. One must shed light on those confines beyond which it only sees enemies. One must explore the outer fringes to which it exiles the men, ideas and morals it does not want.

A culture does not want what makes it afraid. The history of political morals thus leads back to a perennial inventory of the defences which the custodians of power have compiled in response to their fears, headed by fear of the poor, the idle, the loners, the mad, the non-conformists, the rebels, the young and the women.

None of these fears are 'natural' to man. All have been taught him.

The collective phobia against sex is even less a part of human nature than the others. Our nature is animal, and our sexuality a form of innate courage. What psychoanalysis discovers within us – dread, hypocrisy, subconscious disgust and apology – are the changing products of a terrorism over our minds and bodies exerted by the powers of society (State, Church, family) before we reach the age of discretion.

Whether the effects of these shocks are perpetuated through immemorial inheritance (as Jung believed, or each individual childhood re-enacts a primitive genesis myth (Freud), is of little importance. Suffice to say that the aim of those who inflict these 'moral' scars upon us is not our instruction but our ignorance.

No civilization was founded upon knowledge: every civilization is born barbaric. Whatever a culture *is* it owes to chance. Whatever it is *not* it owes to the will.

To whose will, though, if not that of those who make sure they have the monopoly on prohibition? Distinguishing between men or women, depriving some of the rights granted to others, exterminating or exiling those whom one has first despoiled, are the first moves of a hierarchic organization through which a tribal horde learns to conform. They remain the first concerns of a democracy that gives itself laws.

The citizens of Athens, reunited in the body politic (from which slaves and foreigners were excluded) spent the best part of their time in public office ostracizing whoever among them looked as if he were thinking for himself. The Chilean concentration camps or the Soviet psychiatric clinics are the intellectual descendants of such customs.

Violent elimination of dissidents, however, is a costly procedure and history teaches us that the outcome is risky. A more reliable method consists therefore of ensuring that no one gets ideas other than those serving to perpetuate power. The ABC of conservatism is based upon the permanent control of power. And no surer means have ever been found of exercising this control than censorship for the masses.

How long, I asked at the start of this essay, will works of art continue to be threatened with the stake? How long will producers serving the bourgeois power structure go on trying to stultify those images created by their directors' poetic need? How long will they suppress – or translate into their insipid jargon – the texts into which their scenarists and scriptwriters have tried to put their views on love, happiness and all that is new? Alas, for a long time to come, I fear!

For a long, long time . . . For as long, no doubt, as authors and artists don't resign themselves to respecting the grammar of the State. For as long as these incorrigible rebels won't agree to make believe but prefer to pass on wisdom. For as long as these storytellers of the future aren't content to harp always on the same well-worn themes but try to describe life with newly minted words. For as long as these unconscious moralists place their honour and pride in their creation above its profitability. For as long, finally, as these eternal spoilsports prefer intelligence to fame, beauty to money, nudity to disguise, adventure to order, challenge to calculation and dreams to trickery. We might as well say for ever.

Ugliness, boredom and war

I am often asked for a definition of pornography. So many other people have given one without managing to reach a common agreement that I have deliberately avoided speaking out until now. But it so happens that I've just been to see something (and many of you will have seen it before me, for it has acquired classic status) which for want of a better term I consider pornographic. All of a sudden I glimpsed a possible new meaning of this ambiguous word.

The pornographic film to which I am referring is none other than Ingmar Bergman's *Scenes from Married Life*.

So as not to have to mention them again, let us immediately dispose of the *visually* obscene aspect of this film – the least of its faults, I'd say, taking into account the seriousness of the others. I call obscene, in this case, the scenes in which the protagonists, Johan and Marianne, husband and wife, are supposed to be making love.

To start with they always do it fully dressed. Fully dressed is putting things mildly: buttoned up to the collar! So uptight and dowdy in their attire that one just can't see how they manage to achieve any sort of contact other than with zips and flies.

The director's intention was probably to illustrate the difficulty his characters had in communicating, Right. But I maintain that to get this across he used pornographic means of expression. This he did not only by posing this cocooned couple one on top of the other, but by making them employ gestures so ugly and graceless he probably put people off lovemaking for months.

That's the very word for which I was unwittingly searching: ugliness. *Pornography is love and sex made ugly*. Courteline said that 'modesty consists of hiding what is not beautiful'.

Making love fully clothed is not at all unaesthetic in itself: I am only taking Bergman to task for using this gimmick in order to render the amorous conduct of his lovers repellent.

The grotesque little gasps he makes them emit have the same intention: to bring physical pleasure, the sexual instinct and finally love, into disrepute.

To tell the truth, I am indulging in improper – and quite pointless – reflection when attributing this or that intention to the director. I oughtn't to give a damn about his intentions: the only thing that counts is the effect on the spectator. And this effect, so far as I'm concerned, leaves no room for doubt. Johan and Marianne's embraces (if that's what one can call their furtive straddlings) made me feel *ashamed*.

When a 'love' scene makes those who watch it feel ashamed, isn't one right to call it pornographic? Which is what I'm doing.

Maybe my modesty is too far removed from the famous 'common decency' for me to be allowed to dwell upon it, but I wasn't alone when seeing this film and I'm happy to say that my revulsion was shared by all those with me. You might object that they were people of similar opinions. Well, in a certain sense, perhaps, but I've never claimed to speak for the Roman Catholic Church nor to represent the bourgeois State, either: I'm simply the humble spokesman for those for whom sensual pleasure is a good thing.

I've never been able to work out (although I realize I've not exactly exerted myself here) whether Bergman usually looks at sexuality with sympathy or horror: his ideas are on the whole so involved that they bore me.

The over-intrusive fear of the Deity in his work has anyhow helped dissuade me from studying it. Now that this director seems to have been cured of his mystical dread, it is unfortunately all too obvious that he has become afraid of real humanity. It's clear the man lives in a permanent state of panic. I'm very sorry for him, but don't see why I should pay to watch the indecent display of his phobias.

Indecent? Here of course I return to my theme: the film didn't only seem to me pornographic because it made sex ugly, but it embarrassed me particularly because the director had to work so hard to make love ugly. First he degrades physical love, as I've just noted, then too the love which is said to come from the heart, but which I prefer to see as a function of the mind.

The story deals with a husband and wife who would really like to love each other but don't succeed in doing so and separate, seeing each other again from time to time – and that's where things go wrong and become straight porn. For these two failures, who profess to know each other well, have the nerve to hold up their flabby, drab, dismal, embittered and resigned feelings as the very model of what they persist in calling love.

As they haven't been able to succeed socially, professionally or domestically these people, whose lives need not have been so mediocre, 'obscenify' love by trying their best to make us believe that this bond is – essentially, everywhere, and for ever – a form of mediocrity; worse, mediocrity incarnate, the archetype of absolute mediocrity. Each stage of this couple's ageing process is there to convince us that 'there's nothing we can do', that everyone is and always will be 'like that'.

Has Bergman made this statement about impotence in order to deplore it? No, he licks his lips: love's mediocrity, he proclaims in the film, is all to the good.

If this work had goaded me to some violent reaction,

I'd have considered the director's provocation salutary: the artist is not forbidden to evoke unhappiness, pettiness, folly, and banality, so he can instruct, pity, scare or even amuse. But his demonstration here didn't rouse my indignation or make me laugh: it bored me.

So from this experience I've drawn a second definition: *a spectacle is pornographic if it presents love and sex as boring*.

Examining my two definitions more closely, they seemed to overlap, since boredom is a form of ugliness and ugliness ought always to bore us.

The intimate interplay between ugliness and boredom isn't confined to the stage or screen alone. Every day I see it thriving, everywhere I look, in the way people dress, make themselves up, furnish their homes, and fail to enjoy themselves. In this respect our western society seems to be right in the middle of one of its frequent silly seasons.

The miniskirt era represented an outbreak of intelligence; the current fad for old cast-offs undoubtedly constitutes an episode of mass stupidity.

Thinking about the reason for this freak of fashion, I came to the worrying realization that periods of bad taste in dress, for over a century at least, have regularly preceded major wars.

This correlation isn't of course a random one. Nations accept war more readily when they are bored. And they are never so bored as when pleasure in beauty and love is denied them. The naked thighs of girls in the streets might perhaps have finally diverted men from their old passion for destruction, murder and mutual suicide. The subconscious frustration caused by long skirts and farthingales comes just at the right time to restore to men those manly virtues the economists and strategists need in order to manipulate and remould the masses.

I hope I'm only exaggerating, but I'm not really sure I am. It seems ominous to me that ugly fashions, debased love, the flesh denied, and pleasure denigrated coincide with the conspicuous nostalgia for Nazi brutalities and other horrors with which the cinema and comic strips have regaled us for the last few years. It seems all of a piece. You start by lengthening skirts; you 'remember' as Mr Bergman so obligingly does, that human love isn't worth the candle; you 'recall' as Signora Liliana Cavani and Monsieur Louis Malle have so imaginatively done, that the days of totalitarianism and war weren't, for sadomasochists with strong stomachs, too bad after all. And you wind up making the bored countries wish for those times to return.

The alternative, 'make love not war', is not as naïve as the hippy-bashers would have us believe. If love is rotten, war is nice. If sex bores us, war will distract us!

A final definition then, the most serious and gravest in implication: *every spectacle that puts love and sex in the service of war is pornographic.*

In the long run this simple rule ought to be the only criterion to which our censors (if they aren't themselves warmongers and morticians) could profitably refer.

Does this mean that I, Emmanuelle Arsan of all people, am calling for censorship? Well, for once, yes! War is the only one of man's activities against which every sort of prejudice and violence is legitimate.

Conservative pornography and revolutionary eroticism

No breast is quite as disturbing as the bosom of Eros.

As long as the bourgeoisie thought eroticism to be conservative, it was respected while pornography was suppressed. This tradition has just been reversed: eroticism has recently been recognized in France as being an enemy of the regime, while pornography is encouraged.

This observation might seem surprising, for it goes against appearances: how can I claim that political power favours pornography after the government and Parliament have loudly condemned it? There'll always be the collectors, who'll pay any price for those banned engravings. Ideas, on the other hand, always seem too dear: producers and the public think twice before paying extra for a film which questions accepted ideas and claims to help change morality and life. Classifying such a film as 'X' isn't just a question of hiding a breast that's already been seen or a pubis familiar to all: it means trying in panic to protect married couples, fathers and mothers of families and their children-to-be, from realizable hopes they haven't yet had, intelligible dreams they haven't yet dared dream. The aim of the new censorship isn't to forbid sensual feeling but to repress mental stimulus. 'Bad citizenship,' as a French Secretary of State for Culture once said, 'must no longer be traced back to the exhibitionist exposing himself, but to the artist's *intention.*' Art will only be tolerated now if it forgoes obscene *thoughts*, i.e. those which the ruling class hasn't thought of first.

It seems that authorities and I are talking different languages altogether. In order that those words which have been annexed by authority aren't lost to us for ever, I therefore suggest that from now on we call pornographic any subject or spectacle which does not question institutions and embarrass the self-righteous. And henceforth let us reserve the term erotic art for those formulations and situations created by us in freedom, which so disturb the ruling ideology that it would rather muffle them with silence.

The pseudo-permissiveness of the bourgeoisie itself would thus rightly be recognized as pornographic. By assumption, authority can only allow what confirms and reinforces it: the idea of a bourgeois authority which could stand for being discredited and put at risk is in itself absurd.

During the recent period of so-called sexual permissiveness the ruling class has in fact only authorized freedoms of expression and image which would not threaten its real interests, i.e. its economic circumstances, indeed often serving them, and which did not propose a moral and social solution to replace its own secret ideology.

The secret ideology of bourgeois power is that of war. So the institutions which this power cannot allow to be questioned are those which serve to educate the people for war: the traditional marriage, for example.

The state of matrimony, the concubinage which apes it, as well as their accredited failures (jealousy making the best of the change of partners, provided one stays in fashionable society; silent adulteries; avenging fidelity and infidelity avenged; collusion and rivalry; and divorce itself, that mainstay of an end to marriage as likely as defeat at the end of the war) are patriotic in so much as they do not only harden one to the carnage but also seduce citizens into the consumer society. Their modus operandi is just one more of those which make us their submissive clients. The phases of this method move from desire of the object to its acquisition as private property, from enjoyment to rejection, from usury to disgust and despair. In short, these institutions put capitalism within reach of everyone's pockets. What could be better for making mankind forget that it has other, latent powers?

But marriage, the family, heredity, the generation gap and other means of segregation and isolation aren't the only available schooling for war and economics. To those bored by this domestic pedagogy, the approved fashion currently offers alternatives: the sadism of nostalgia (*The Night Porter*) or that of the drawing-room (like *The Story of O*). In these useful entertainments, woman, beaten, chained, stabbed or pierced is shown to be happy with her destined lot, her nature as a mere receptacle. The civilized man, the cultured male leads her back to her domestic animality and her difference. And since when have civilized people loved what is different from themselves?

In order to be convincing, the economy of war needs racism. Sexual racism isn't satisfied with humiliating every other human being (the half of mankind which doesn't know how to piss against walls): it goes looking for shameful differences, among apparent equals. Some people already consider it quite all right to isolate reds, gays and dykes in moral and verbal ghettos: society, were it less tender-hearted, could just as well have exterminated them; it didn't worry about that sort of thing in the old days. And what if those days returned? We've become too squeamish to burn deviants in the marketplace, but our looks and words are quite capable of burning them by degrees.

Can eroticism do anything to change morality? And why can't pornography? To understand this antithesis one simply has to compare what each proposes and the styles used. Pornography never invents: it lives upon repetition, conformity and compromise. As for the eroticism of ideas, this is not so much permissive as promissive.

What eroticism promises is more sincerity, generosity and gaiety. It means working to organize a world in which inequality between lover and beloved gradually disappears. A world where love and sex don't add arbitrary, useless and avoidable barriers to the inexorable limits we find in Nature. A freedom we'll know how to use.

What would one actually do? Spend the time doing nothing but making love? Isn't there any more to think about than dreaming up new positions? In that case, where would we find the time and place for reading, listening to music, or stargazing – we women who'd always have some man on top of us or under us? And where would the men find enough sperm for so many orgasms?

Let us answer these absurdities simply by saying that the future of love doesn't depend upon physical positioning in the sex act, but on communication between the lovers. Love's future also depends upon relationships of interest and understanding which the society of lovers succeeds in establishing with the rest of the world.

Coitus and myth are not the objectives of eroticism. Eroticism's objective is the mental and social ethos which aims at transforming sexuality and love into sources of knowledge, creativity and evolution, so that the prospect of a happy society may become less utopian.

In a word, eroticism is not sexual, it is amorous. In that too it is the opposite of pornography. Pornography in fact begins when love and sex are presented as antagonistic choices. In the pornographic view of things, people have no existence outside their sex lives. To the erotic way of thought, on the contrary, the most interesting thing is not people's sex lives but people.

People's sexual peccadilloes then have scarcely more than an aesthetic importance. Their sex might be male or female, young or old, black or white, talkative or silent, generous or mean, homeloving or adventurous, exogamous or incestuous: these are certainly quite interesting differences, but they don't need to be subjected to the rigours of the law. Or else one might as well regiment the colour of the eyes, the softness of the skin, the style of jeans one wears. No doubt that'll come in due course, should someone want to suppress eroticism.

Repression is what makes us all sexually obsessed. This childishness takes us through infancy. Eroticism's challenge to this mentally backward state is in wanting to help us grow by making sexual obsession pointless. We will only be really intelligent, free and capable of unselfishness when we don't have to place so much emphasis on copulation.

At present we only believe in having lovers because the totalitarian society of our husbands and wives prevents our having friends. And we do desperately need friends, people that is, with whom we are free to talk about ideas we daren't have, actions we daren't perform, places we daren't go, people we daren't get to know, dreams we daren't dream, sadnesses we can't explain.

Our fear of confiding our fears to others is far greater than our sexual timidity. All too often we make love only because we haven't the courage to do anything bolder.

If eroticism to many people is still involved with sexual demands, and primarily struggles against the barriers an antique morality erects between bodies, that isn't out of sordid materialistic passion, but because the body is mind, heart and dream. To be interested in others' bodies, to cross the space separating us from them, to fill the emptiness of space with vital time, is not to want to take another's belongings, nor to consume a human being like a commodity – it means wanting to know them, to become capable of understanding and loving them.

Eroticism, in short, is not based upon anything more or less revolutionary than this hypothesis: learning to love is as feasible as continuing to learn to kill.

The revolutionaries would have made some objective progress were they to recognize that true eroticism is not a diversionary ideology destined to distract one from serious matters, but rather the contrary, that it is the concept which will liberate us from obsession with sex so that we can at last think about something else.

We shall never be in a position to win freedom and dignity in our working relationships if we don't simultaneously try to make our amorous relationships free and dignified. Let us declare then that if we sincerely wish to build a new world that love is a main priority, just as much as social justice, knowledge and freedom. In place of the marriage of domination and exploitation let us substitute a still unknown relationship, 'man's pleasure in man', without which, said Albert Camus, 'the world would remain an immense solitude'.

No political set-up has any sense unless it is accompanied by a new ideology of love: an ideology for adults, not protected minors; an ideology in the image of the society we feel capable of inventing: liberating, responsible, trusting, refreshing and fair.

To take us further along this road. I suggest that from now on we reserve the word erotic for everything that goes on in an atmosphere free from prejudice, solitude or fear.

The pornography of power has not, one realizes, much in common with such a wish. The instrument of conservatism and instant profit, it deliberately reinforces the fear of sex, so that we do not aspire to cure ourselves of other habits. That, for example, of allowing ourselves to be exploited.

V. Routes and Ruins in Sand

Must I undress, My Lord?

To each his schizophrenia! Anonymity is mine.

I don't make a show of my horror of publicity as though it were a virtue: knowing that it makes me conspicuous and isolates me within a society in which sales-talk is a moral obligation, I confess it like a perversion.

Exposing my identity to the interviewer or photographer causes me the same sort of pain as light streaming into the eyes of an albino. To brag about this physical indisposition would, however, seem to me as absurd as being vain about the colour of my hair.

I even admit that my taste for shadow and silence makes me incomprehensible to those born with the thirst for fame. I resign myself to the harshness of a world obsessed with categories and conformity, when men and women with black skins seem to be of a different species to those who are white; a world where the old cannot understand the young; where those who dream of power despise those tired of violence; where women expect to bring life and men believe they can deal death; a world in which man has become past and woman has remained future.

So I don't expect this world to understand me better if I hide. Yet I know I'll be misunderstood all the more if I reveal myself. Not because I am hopelessly different from others, but simply because I am another. We are all terrified of other people.

Why then do we pretend to be interested in them? Because we are also strangers to ourselves, and a conversation with our image in the mirror frightens us.

In order to escape this solitude we could make real

friends, friends in spirit and flesh. But the retreat into fiction seems safer to us because fantasy is not binding.

Political illusionists, preachers of unimportant religions, prophets of improbable misfortunes, thus become our daily companions, boon companions since we have no obligations towards them.

This abstract confidence we have in them doesn't mean, though, that we expect them to honour their commitments any more than we do. Nobody in our dying culture asks for words to be followed by deeds. In the civilization of words, the word can no longer be kept. The only rule which remains inexorable is one's duty to keep up appearances.

Decked out in their artistic livery, authors and actors more than anyone are entrusted to maintain such appearances. Not only are they expected to glorify good form, but to show with a stylish flourish and unwearying smile the gratitude they feel for their mannequin roles.

In our feudal society the public's interest thus imposes a permanent obligation upon the artist. Who is expected to be a slave to an entertainment the public applauds. With every success which he grants that public, he must renounce a little more of his freedom.

One of his obligations is to bare his private life to the public. The good artist must constantly maintain the submissive posture of the villager's daughter in the film *The War Lord*, who had no other role to fulfil except that of kneeling before Charlton Heston and saying 'Shall I undress, My Lord?'

I'll be told I'm kicking up too much of a fuss over such a trifling threat to freedom: the public's curiosity isn't necessarily an inquisition for the artist, and as everyone has known for years the artist's function is incompatible with his right to keep his private life private. Writing, it will be asserted, means laying open one's morals and character quite as much as one's work. To take part in a film is to risk disapproval for oneself as well as for one's role. To be an actor is to accept displaying oneself, clothed or naked, offstage as much as on. How can one in all good faith engage in these media activities and claim anonymity?

It seems my critics have forgotten that Homer and Shakespeare hid so completely behind their pseudonyms that we still don't know who they really were. Any more than we know the names of most of those who have populated the earth with marble Venuses, bronze Buddhas and wooden Christs. Any more than one can say with any certainty who built the Greek, Khmer or Mayan temples.

I don't really see why the contemporary actor or author should feel bound to display his wounds in public, any more than his precursors did. The actor in particular is by definition one who tries to give life to a character different from himself. He effaces himself for the fictitious character he portrays. For the duration of the role he forgets who he really is so that – for the duration of the dream – someone else can exist.

In my view he succeeds in this all the better by avoiding being too well known in everyday life.

I've already stated (it's one of my preoccupations and I'm not repeating myself by accident) that whoever writes ought, for his part, only to be concerned with the characters he brings into the world. Inventing them and loving them is enough to honour his name and justify his life. He has no need to add his own portrait to theirs.

More than ever, I think that a writer, director, painter or actor each has a right to the great name of artist when they ask to be judged by what they do rather than by what they are.

Whenever they reveal themselves at the same time as their work, they are not behaving like artists but objects. Those of them who go along with this alienation may be real creators: sometimes they also make good puppets, but ones who no longer have control of their own strings. When the performance is over and the farce is at an end, they find themselves alone as objects always are.

Am I abnormal if pulling the strings of invented characters gives me more pleasure than acting out my own life onstage? Is it an antisocial sin for which I must ask pardon? I know that publishers and readers insist on believing that my novels are autobiographical. Is this really out of interest in me? Or do they think I'm so lacking in imagination as not to know how to invent heroes more intelligent, courageous, and better looking than myself?

I maintain without false modesty that their doubts insult my dignity as an artist. And that counts for more, in my eyes, all things considered, than the popularity I could have acquired through intimate confessions.

To the best of my knowledge I've never posed as a confessional writer, nor an autobiographer, nor a mirror of my times. Therefore I'm justified in asking my times to ignore me.

Yes, I also know I should be more grateful to the social system which feeds me. And I ought to remember that in the world into which I was born, one's first duty is to get rich. I'd be more respected if I knew how to run my reputation like a business, with a publicity budget and a public relations firm. I'd have a more comfortable house and bigger and more luxurious cars. Sure. But would I be happier – which means freer? And would I feel prouder?

Famous, I'd certainly leave an inheritance. Anonymous, perhaps I'll leave a name . . .

Continuing?

When the holidays are over, do we have any other prospect than to resume our former functions and old habits? Is any other possibility open to us except just to take up our everyday lives and humdrum routines exactly where we left off? From lost springs to disenchanted autumns shall we continue reeling off our allotted span in this way, like spiders spinning their webs, without ever changing the pattern instead of deciding at long last that our role is to innovate?

I do know that the majority of human beings have no other desire but *to continue.* Unchanging concerns and aims, repetition of thought and act: these seem guarantees of security. And security tempts most men and women more than happiness.

But I haven't forgotten either that the only future the characters in Jean-Paul Sartre's *In Camera* can imagine is expressed by the play's last line of dialogue: 'Very well then, let's continue!' – and that these characters are residents of Hell! . . .

If we ourselves have no ambition other than to exist without change, we cannot then complain that our existences are, in the precise sense of the word, infernal. For no one – neither men nor gods – condemned us to this hell: we confined ourselves here voluntarily.

One bright idea of Christian theology which has always seemed admirable to me is this: when a believer dies, he doesn't go before a divine tribunal to be judged, but himself judges his life with complete objectivity for the first time and spontaneously chooses to go to Heaven, Purgatory or Hell, according to his merits.

However, eternity is a very convenient excuse for those who have always been frightened of living. It would be better if we tried to exercise our spirit of equity and clairvoyance in this world: to please ourselves, for example, and give pleasure to others rather than deferring our reward and theirs by speculating upon the Beyond.

But how can we know what is for our own good and how can we be sure of what is good for others?

Nowhere does there exist an absolute criterion of value. The value of an action depends on how successful it is. In other words we can justifiably consider we are acting well whenever we effectively adjust our behaviour so as to attain the result we seek. Conversely, we are imbeciles and deserve our unhappiness if we desire something yet do everything not to achieve it.

I do think, however, that we devote the best part of our time to the latter . . .

If I gave credit to the Church earlier I am wary of the moral rules it imposes on daily life. This morality and its rules are in fact based upon a single simple principle: *all desire is bad*. The satisfaction of desire is always an evil, the intelligence we use in getting what we want is necessarily perverted, and the pleasure, however transitory, which we feel when achieving our desires will be paid for with eternal torment.

The Christian Hell is thus opposed to the existentialist, or humanist, hell. The latter punishes us throughout our earthly lives for our fearful desires, lazy imaginations and lack of courage in pursuing the satisfaction of our desire. God's Hell, in contrast, watches over those who seek further knowledge and want always to know 'something else'. It traps all those curious for the unknown. It is reserved for those who collect experiences or who seek novelty, and for those pure spirits for whom no fruit of this world can plainly be forbidden.

To sum up, our destiny is clear: there is no Heaven anywhere for anybody; we only have a choice between two Hells.

As far as I'm concerned, I've never said anything except the following: we have to decide which of these hells scares us least – and choose to believe in one or the other from now on. When we're dead it'll be too late.

Should we be depressed by this situation? Am I a pessimist? Of course not! The proposed choice is ridiculously facile and ought to delight our inexhaustible sense of humour, because *one of these two hells does not exist*! God's Hell is as imaginary as eternal life. We only really need fear hell on this Earth.

I am not writing this in order to indulge in polemic against the Church. Others have done that and will doubtless go on doing so, certainly better than I. And yet it seems their efforts don't amount to very much: men believe and go on believing because they *want* to believe, not because anyone obliges them to.

And while on this subject I don't want to hear some pedant hold forth about social environment. The archaeology of the psyche and the human condition turn into religion whenever they make us all the creatures and playthings of invisible powers – History with a capital H replacing God – and thus reintroduce transcendance into our lives. This modern faith is an alibi which no more excuses our submission to fate than could primitive belief, in the eyes of science. All faith horrifies me and I do not write in order to suffer.

. . . What in fact do I write for? Why *continue* to write, when I see that continuity is diabolical?

I just wrote that learned disputes about the existence or non-existence of God, the Devil and Eternity convince nobody and are therefore pointless. I also know perfectly well that my books and articles – no more or less, anyway, than everything else that appears in this field – have never succeeded in persuading anyone at all that he causes himself needless and absurd pain by being jealous and possessive in love, by masturbating with shame and remorse, and by not daring to sample fully and joyously the many mental and physical excitements, solitary or shared, public or private, which can do nobody harm, least of all himself.

The statistics I've read all seem to indicate that the views of adolescents about love, pleasure, marriage, and freedom are more or less identical with the views of their elders twenty years previously. Similarly the reactions of the vast majority of men and women faced with what they unsympathetically go on calling 'premarital sex', 'adultery', 'homosexuality', 'orgies', 'incest', 'perversions', 'pornography', etc., are no different after an alleged 'sexual revolution' from what they were almost a quarter of a century before it. So what can one hope for?

No doubt it will be said that I am exaggerating or mistaken. It will be pointed out to me that eroticism reigns over literature, photography and the plastic arts; that the press gives space to sex and nudity every day; that women can now freely display their breasts upon beaches and their entire bodies on some of those beaches; that there's hardly a stage play in which an actor doesn't at some point appear in his birthday suit; and that the cinema (although the special target of official prudery and the much-maligned victim of self-censorship and producer's idiocy) is at last showing 'almost' everything. Each day we are promised that television will soon follow in its wake.

Possibly. Yet do real people live more freely than they used to? Do they think more boldly, intelligently or objectively? Do they experience pleasures they never knew before? Are they happier together? Or have freedom, conviviality and awareness increased only among writers, journalists, photographers, actors and directors – amongst those that is, who have anyhow always been or wanted to be, different?

And don't these 'artists', as others often call them with condescending and sceptical tolerance, write, invent, exhibit and portray ultimately only for themselves, in order to amuse each other without really having the slightest influence on 'outside' society or prevailing morality?

What's more, doesn't asking this question constitute one more exercise in futility? In fact everyone knows that there are as many answers to every sociological problem as there are people able to open their mouths. I'm quite sure I'd find just as many readers ready to demonstrate the decisive role played by art and literature in the evolution of social behaviour and moral ideas as I would be willing to prove the pointlessness of such means.

If I gradually find myself lacking the courage to write, it's because the hypothesis of the futility of words is very much in my mind. I'll never know for sure whether this is right or wrong, nor will anyone else.

Why then, once again, am I writing? Is it because railing against 'words' is for every writer, as for Sartre, an affectation which commits him to nothing? A futile obsession with his trade?

I don't feel any more able now to convert others than I ever did. Nor did I want to do so. I've never felt any vocation to be a missionary, nor do I see myself as a militant. Only those who already think as I do and who've always shared my beliefs and life-style assure me that I give them pleasure by saying aloud what they like to hear; by writing what they like to read; by keeping them company and letting them know they are not alone in the world, not isolated and damned by all. So perhaps writing is nothing more than an act of friendship.

Is it a duty too? Whenever I stop writing my friends reproach me for taking advantage of their friendship without doing anything to deserve it. Ought they to be the only ones working to make me happy?

They remind me of what I've already said in their name and mine: 'I do dream, but I don't expect my dreams to become reality. I know no fear or hope and thus am free. To whoever desires without fear or hope, all things are possible.'

My friends argue that if I were to become silent and disillusioned, that would mean that I had been unwittingly hopeful. If I were to stop writing because my dreams weren't realized, it would be because I had faith in them without knowing it. If I stopped talking to others, it would be because their ideas and actions subconsciously scared me.

In this way my friends make me understand that keeping silent would be to deny myself. They think I should 'continue'.

Continue? Like Jean-Paul Sartre's damned?

Or are there forms of perseverance which don't pave the road to hell? Is writing ceaselessly and without respite the only possible way the writer has of seeking the new? Has he no other chance of finding that 'somewhere else' which his intuition makes him sense without telling him where it is? And must he accept that continuity in order to be allowed endless variety?

Perhaps. Doesn't this theory, simply because I've thought it up, oblige me to renounce a part of my freedom? Yet that's what everyone does who chooses to love. To love is to be disturbed.

Also, of course, to disturb others! The writer who renounces the freedom of being alone does not know how to live without involving others.

This last assurance ought at least to enlighten me on one score: a world in which one lives for making others live will never be a hell.

Sixty-Nine

In Sweden and Denmark, in towns where I've never been before and where no one knows me, I was recently given rooms at two successive hotels with the identical number, 69.

The coincidence delights me. As with love, a journey is successful only when it's a game. The real routes are those which open the mouth and the sex and divert you towards the sand.

I love being fucked in the mouth like one fucks the sand. To be a beach licked by tongues of sea. Pricks like to come into the sand of beaches. Cunts like being caressed by seaweed.

The sex converges upon the mouth because love looks for knowledge. Knowledge, the game and the climax need numbers. 69 is a wise number, a figure which brings the players luck and a code which makes a dialogue of desire.

Knowledge only makes advances when desire serves as its spur. Even the most detached researcher really only seeks enjoyment. To come upon a solution or pursue some line of study is no less of a luxury and pleasure than enjoying having one's sex kissed.

To kiss a sex, however, is open to a greater number of people. *Soixante-neuf* is not an élitist pastime but one that does exemplify an idea. Its finality is more intellectual than physical. It is a method of discovery, an exploratory attitude, a theory one seeks to prove, as much for its random developments as for its known merits.

If I didn't worry about appearing pretentious, I wouldn't hesitate to attribute to this practice virtues known as 'heuristic': by which logicians designate formulations whose veracity one doesn't try to establish immediately but which are adopted as guidelines in the search for a truth. Since the day belongs to entertainment rather than epistemological analysis I'm going to try to clarify the more immediately demonstrable qualities and aspirations of the *soixante-neuf*.

Firstly its artistic nature is clearly evident. When facing two inverted bodies who does not think of a work whose sculptor has been filled with symmetry and balance and is sure of the moving beauty of his vision? It would be safe to bet that the forgotten Taoist who thousands of years ago had the idea of depicting the intimate space of the universe by the *tai-ki* was more involved with figurative art than physics or metaphysics.

To the artist harmony is, incontestably, more of a spiritual, emotional and moral asset than a biological one. So there's nothing surprising about the *soixante-neuf* being a privileged example of equality and synchrony between the sexes. This conjunction divides, with unparalleled fairness, the egoism that seeks climax and the altruism that wants to induce climax. Each partner offers the other a mutual pleasure to be enjoyed simultaneously: this is a rare rule.

So the *soixante-neuf* is tender, since the care its practitioners take in their mutual attentions is a supreme act of love.

The *soixante-neuf* is a relationship between equal and interchangeable partners. All that is required is for one participant to be superposed upon the other. This is one circumstance where Ovid's observation in *The Art of Love* is wonderfully relevant: 'Venus has a thousand ways of disporting herself, but the simplest and least tiring is to remain half-reclining on one's right side.' (It has always seemed to me, though, that the left side would do just as well.) And in either case Venus's lover cannot but adopt the same posture and thus reflect its asexual narcissism in a blurred and disturbing mirror.

Yes, asexual. The *soixante-neuf* is the least sexist embrace there is. However sensitive she may be, no feminist should refuse. This method of making love doesn't even require the sexes of its performers to be different. A *soixante-neuf* can be just as successful in form and as satisfying in effect whether practised by a man and a woman, two men or two women together, or any other combination.

Better still, since there is no penetration involved there is less chance of physical incompatibility.

Another advantage is that the *soixante-neuf* is eminently humanitarian and public-spirited at a time when the population explosion threatens the world with a prolonged return to barbarism. This technique is more certainly contraceptive than the Pill, does not expose one to the trauma of abortion and, moreover, has probably never caused any wars.

Its peaceable virtues probably stem from the fact that the *soixante-neuf* is neither fanatical in principle nor limited in option. It doesn't rule out the coexistence of tastes: its practitioners are inquisitive about every new experience and avid for new combinations.

The *soixante-neuf* is in fact the most normal preparation for exploring the 669, the 699, the 696, the 966, the 969 – and many other possible combinations. Its mathematical possibilities are limitless. And the most interesting thing is that one only has to add another digit to each system in order to multiply it tenfold . . . Observe: 666 becomes 6666 and 999 blossoms into 9999. Nothing stops you going further still: one more participant and everybody's pleasure is multiplying a hundredfold; two, and it's heightened a thousand times. You would have to be a puritan indeed to claim after all this that sex is limited.

Intolerance is so foreign to science and real art that no

devotee of *soixante-neuf* sees any objection to people sporting tee-shirts with the number 68 on them. I myself have no axe to grind on this subject, and provided these imaginative characters would be kind enough to explain to me how they manage it, I'd be very pleased to try out their formula. Unless it's simply a question of being hypocritical or timid, who settles for less because they daren't try for more?

Anyway, I won't hold their deviation against them: the greater the mind the fewer the limits. Our world has only one chance of real progress, and that is by allowing everything – the *soixante-neuf*, of course, but not only that. We'll only stop being the cruel savages and ignorant primitives that we are on the day when we stop condemning and persecuting all sexual misfits and minority groups.

Soixante-neuf is after all an intellectual quest. This is a truism: for every activity on earth reflects man's fumbling desire for truth.

None of us would be strictly hetero- or homo-sexual, fetishist or exhibitionist, masturbators or prick teasers, had not the opinions and judgments of others haphazardly herded us into fixed categories and kept us there. We remain labelled as men who love men, women who love animals or solitary outsiders who love objects, because society won't let us look elsewhere for someone perhaps different from us and with whom, maybe, we'll be equal.

For who is foolish enough to set limits on love?

Any experience can give one the taste for its opposite. Every idea can welcome its opposite. There should be no betrayal or ridicule involved in moving from *soixante-neuf* to coitus, from masturbation to troilism, from female arms to male ones – and back again. It oughtn't to be *wrong* to desire everything, to want to experience and try everything.

Will this paradise one day really be ours? It is possible if we finally decide to be free *together*.

For my part, I can only call for this communal freedom. I've learned from the love I've given and received that in order to be happy, being free isn't enough for me: others must be so with me.

Everyone must be free along with me.

Solitude of freedom, like solitude of thought, is suicidal. I don't want to be free so as to die alone, I want to have enough friends so as to be able to live.

I speak and will always speak to all men and women, whether or not they listen to me just as happy lovers sing openly of their reasons for playing the game of life . . . A game which changes with days and ages, bodies and words, sexes and hearts, tears and forgetfulness, but lasts as long as the spirit still goes on questing.

So today, like these lovers, I'll sing about the love of a dusky girl and a blonde: one of them perhaps is myself, the other maybe someone I'm waiting to meet. Two women among millions, but whose encounter will be unique. Two naked women, who could also be a yellow child and a blue bird, a black man and a red flag.

I'll sing so that those who are like me without knowing it will recognize each other in their dreams, and so that those who are different from me will feel less alone.

Dark girl's song

You are blonde and you're like me
When you're naked
My lover!
Your breasts are round like mine,
My breath is hot like yours,
Your heart is mad like mine,
My dream is sweet like yours.

Blonde's song

You are blonde and you're like me
When you love me,
My lover!
I open my womb with your hands,
Teeth sink into my loins,
I'm seduced by your caresses,
I bind you by my promises.

Dark girl's song

Your body is fair and mine is dark:
But the bodies of lovers
Are one!
When my tongue licks your well,
When your sex wets my mouth,
When my throat drinks your desire,
I come through what makes you come.

Blonde's song

You are my night, I am your day!
Twice blessed is
Lovers' love:
When our arms and legs entwine
Making us twice as lovely
We give our other lovers
Twice the reason for being happy.

Naked with you

In Sweden and Denmark I don't only dream about *soixante-neuf* and do it, but I look up old friends of both sexes. That's why there as in in other countries I feel at home.

In my own home I live in the nude. I only feel at ease when I can go around naked, but being naked alone is pointless. To be naked intelligently, happily and erotically means being able to be naked with one's friends.

If my friends didn't like me better nude than dressed, they wouldn't like me at all. If I didn't prefer being naked with them to being naked on my own, I wouldn't like them.

This summer, in the nude with them, I asked them to sing along with me. I wrote this song for them lightheartedly and with their help. Suzanne Brøgger set it to music:

Which of you, my friends
Knows how to see me with the naked eye?
Which of you, my lovers
Strokes me with naked hand?
Which of you, my children
Kisses me with naked lips?
And which of you, my men,
Will love me with naked heart?
If one of you desires me
Nude for him,
I'll be nude for you all,
My friends!

Passing stranger
Who seeks love,
I'm the unknown
Hidden by day
And shown by night.
Lucky one who finds me!
Fearful one who shuns me!
Happy one who tries me
Without too much ceremony,
Without asking me
If I know how to love,
If I love to forget.
What does my name matter?
It's the name of the weather,
The name of life,
The name of a friend,
Singing in the wind
Until it's time.

Which of you, my friends,
Makes love with eyes shut?
Which of you, my lovers,
Strokes with hands closed?
Which of you, my children,
Kisses, lips pursed?
And which of you, my men,
Only makes love in the dark?
If one of you desires
Me to be his wife,
I'll be wife to you all,
My friends!

A naked girl,
So beautifully naked,
Shows her friends
Her belly and breasts,

Strong as life,
Warm as the weather,
Fresh as the wind.
Who loves her touches her
And touches her heart,
Or meets her tongue,
Or clasps her hands,
Or sings her name.
No difference
Between young and old,
Between black and white.
She has so many friends
And loves them so much!
They are her lovers.

Which of you, my friends,
Dreams with me, eyes closed?
Which of you, my lovers,
Plays with me with naked hands?
Which of you, my children,
Loves with me with open heart?
And which of you, my men,
Always lives with reckless heart?

If one of you desires me,
For himself alone,
I'll be alone with you all,
My friends!

The eyes of only one man
Know not how to see.
The hand of only one man
Knows not how to clasp.
The body of only one man
Knows not how to come.
The heart of only one man

Knows not how to love.
Solitary lover
Undressing me
With your eyes closed,
You'd see me better
If others with you
Saw me naked.
Jealous lover,
You'd love me better
If others as well as you
Made love to me, too.

Eyes wide open I see
With which of you, my friends?
Body wide open I come
With which of you, my lovers?
Heart wide open I desire
With which of you, my children?
I'll live true to life,
But with which of you, my men?

If one of you desires me
Dead for him,
I'll be lost to you all,
My friends!

At the end of time,
Girls of the wind
Who like to change
Fire and place,
Faith and law,
Will no longer want
To be naked.
They'll go away,
Far away from your life,
Without explaining themselves,

Without disclosing anything,
Without consoling you,
Without kissing you,
Without dressing you again.

All this just
Because a lover
Doesn't always know
How to make love well.

'Emmanuelle, why don't you have children?'

'Because I couldn't be any use to them.'

'Who is stopping you at least making them happy?'

'Everyone. I don't live on a desert island, nor would I want to.'

'Not even alone with your children?'

'Especially not with them! Children who live alone with their mothers don't learn how to grow up: they only learn to age.'

'If you did have children, wouldn't you like to keep them with you, so that they'd be like you? Would you rather they were like other people?'

'I wouldn't want them to be "like" me or anyone else.'

'Aren't you happy to be what you are?'

'No good comes of imitation. If our world is becoming more and more boring, maybe that's because its inhabitants have no higher ambition than to imitate each other – to the detriment of imagination and sense . . . Nothing makes people happier these days than to be able to say: "I'm like . . . I do as so-and-so does . . ." We live in the era of imitation. Is there any difference today between a Thai political speech and an Argentine military dictator's pronouncement? How does an Iranian bourgeois woman's elegance differ from a Parisienne's? Does a Nairobi nightclub offer different distractions from a Zamboanga discothèque?'

'Do you get nostalgic about times when people and customs were more diverse?'

'I don't waste my time feeling regret for what I've never known. I prefer to look for something else.'

'Aren't you simply advocating change for the sake of it?'

'By changing ourselves we'd take fewer risks than we do by perpetually imitating one another.'

'Must we forget everything we know? Renounce all those things we like doing?'

'Life in society has conditioned us too thoroughly for us to be able to discard our reactions and obsessions. This planet only offers the chance of true social change to children not yet born only on condition, however, that we have nothing to do with their education. The youth of the future will not be born of our senility.'

'Yet it's through the inherited distinguishing features that living species defy the threat of time. For all existing matter, if that matter is capable of thought, time is a frightening variable. Life is a heroic scheme devised to combat the temporal horror of chance. Living is a utopia of invariance. Didn't you yourself somewhere quote a contemporary biologist (Professor François Jacob, Nobel prizewinner in Medicine, writing in *The logic of the living*): "Life never comes to an end: it simply continues"?'

'I don't expect the human race to change shape, but I am sure that it must change beliefs.'

'Isn't that exactly the business of education?'

'Unfortunately the only kind of education we know how to practise is reactionary. We don't teach our children simply to live, but we force them to adopt our materialist values.'

'No society can function without the illusion of security. Morality usually conceals the will to survive.'

'Do all societies have to be immortal? The study of matter tells that before we can rebuild we must first destroy. If human social structures are the most complex and effective in the Universe, that is because they conform to an ever renewable plan which is constantly revised – by death. Immortality would be useless to man's future.'

'Would you like to do away with the untidy prototypes that we are, so that a better organized race could take our place? If so, you ought to applaud the neutron bomb!'

'Genocide and collective suicide have never done any good. Every community that owes its authority to the sword remains haunted by the memory of what it has destroyed. Violence does not build a new world: it reshapes the evil inherent in the old world. Besides, this mechanism works within the consciousness of individuals in the same way as in the collective conciousness. Freud hit the mark when he claimed that our psyche remains scarred by the mythology of the primal horde, whereby the child became a man through the ritual murder of the father and then spent the rest of his life emulating that same tyrannical father. As long as generation after generation adheres to this model of development, mankind will be morally and socially retarded.'

'Would the mother you might have been have prepared her children for this lack of social development?'

'I don't know. I'd at least have tried teaching them kindness.'

'Is it enough for a few to be gentle, in order that mankind may be so too? Christ and the flower-children weren't too successful.'

'I'm not qualified to judge: mysticism and metaphysics are not my forte.'

'Does the optimism I find in your books hide a deep-rooted pessimism?'

'As I am interested neither in demons or angels, I don't predict heaven or hell. The prophets of the apocalypse bore me as much as those who want to save us at all costs. Neither I nor anyone else is able to see that far ahead. I'd be happy if everyone tried to look more closely.'

'At what?'

'At what exists. Instead of inventing ghosts and then being afraid of them.'

'Stop talking in riddles: name these spectres that make your flesh creep.'

'Haven't I discussed them enough already? Haven't I been explicit enough in exposing the mistress who drives the wife mad with jealousy; the virgin bride who becomes the husband's possession; the monogamous couple, who go mad with solitude? Haven't I sufficiently decried prudery, resignation and guilt – all of which make love impossible? Haven't I attacked those moralizing bigots who burn films and books, those wet blankets who lengthen skirts and abhor unfettered breasts, the humourless cops who round up nude bathers and the bloodless judges who lock up open-air fuckers? It's true that these ogres aren't too intelligent, but I'm not obsessed by them. And I wouldn't set out to manipulate the future: not because I am scared of saying too much, but because I know too little.'

'Must parents keep silent, then?'

'Of course!'

'Who, in that case, will preserve our heritage?'

'This heritage is quite capable of preserving itself! It doesn't need our theorizing. Our arts and sciences express history better than we know how. And better than we'll ever know. Children don't learn what mankind is capable of merely by listening to their elders talk: they learn by opening their eyes and ears, and by cultural studies. Let them freely satisfy their curiosity through science and the arts. In time they themselves may then reach out still further.'

'Shouldn't we hide anything from our children?'

'Yes: our war memorials and our battle-songs. On the other hand don't let's hide from them the purpose of love or what love can achieve. Children who are deprived of beauty and goodness take a dislike to the world and thereafter see evil everywhere.'

'So one shouldn't protect them from anything, even from what society judges to be obscene?'

'Society begins by wanting to protect children, women and the elderly. It classifies them by age and sex, according to their alleged innocence or their assumed weakness. Then it ends up excluding them. Children, women and old people don't need protectors, they need people to love them.'

'It isn't true then that you'd have nothing to offer your children, Emmanuelle. You'd only give them the example of love.'

'I don't believe in the usefulness of example.'

'Nor even in the usefulness of ideas?'

'Oh yes. Our ideas are worth more than we are. We, who are relative newcomers to this planet, aren't necessarily happy, good, just, bold, or wise, nor do we have infallible perception, but we've still been able to express happiness, generosity, reason, freedom and beauty.'

'So – works of art, dreams of love, and a passion for ideas: that, finally, is a rich enough inheritance to ensure that our children have enough to live on!'

The half regained

(story)

> **I miss my half-loaf! I love that half-loaf, it used to make me happy.**
>
> ***Sunday, Bloody Sunday***

Andreas was talking philosophy to me while I was making love to his wife. Every so often I would have some difficulty asking him a question or answering his: Malini's cunt was so hot, so urgent that I had to grit my teeth so as not to come too soon. Luckily my interest in what Andreas had to say was helping me resist the impulse of an immediate climax.

Malini doesn't want anything to do with the pill or any other means of contraception. Those first days I would pull out of her just in time, out of consideration for Andreas. Now I no longer hold back. The pleasure I get from ejaculating deep inside her, right up her womb, is too great for me to dream of depriving myself of it. She'll soon be pregnant without any of us knowing for sure whether her husband's sperm or mine has impregnated her.

Andreas asked me abruptly:

'Would you prefer it if my child had been sired by you?'

I said I would. Then Andreas assured me that until Malini became pregnant he would take care only to come in her mouth, anus or on to her belly.

To tell the truth, the idea of such sharing would probably not have come from me. Suddenly however, the prospect of having a baby by Malini with Andreas as its father, seemed to me wholly reasonable. He was better suited than I to face up to the responsibilities a birth implies: the care a child needs, its upbringing and education. For my part I could come even more copiously and pleasurably when making love to Malini by thinking of the consequences that such pleasure would have within her and for the three of us.

'Do you think you'll stay Malini's lover for long?' Andreas asked.

'Yes,' I told him. 'I've never known anyone who was such a good fuck.'

'Man or woman?' Andreas went on.

'Men are usually better than women,' I agreed, 'but your wife is an exception. I wonder why though?'

'Perhaps you've never had a virgin?' he speculated.

'Malini was no longer a virgin when I fucked her for the first time,' I observed.

'She almost was. As you know, she didn't lose her virginity until the night before. And then, well, only half-way.'

Why had he waited until the night before their marriage to take her virginity? Why had he only partially ruptured her hymen? When I met them, during the reception after their return from the church, Malini herself was loudly asking the priest who had just officiated at the wedding ceremony the very same questions. He would nod his head by way of response and continue eating cake.

That day I too questioned Malini's mother on the subject. She spent the next hour telling me in detail about the banal courtship of Andreas and his fiancée. Their meeting had in every respect conformed with the conventions of a cheap novelette: even in the fact that he was in his first year as a teacher while she, his pupil, was in her last year at school. The age difference between them was no less predictable, exactly ten years. Their social background, tastes, minds and language were as happily matched as their good looks.

Had Andreas been younger and more impressionable, I'd certainly have tried to seduce him before her. But he didn't give me any encouragement so I went on staring at Malini.

The priest was as absorbed as I, seeing her naked beneath her long dress. There wasn't any question here of a fleeting, half-glimpsed nudity, merely some happy accident of back-lighting and a chance silhouette of parted legs: this was an open and intentional nakedness which shadow made still more explicit. A nudity whose details were exposed and which imposed themselves in memorable and unexpected abundance.

Thus not only were Malini's breasts quite visible through her absolutely transparent gown, but the opening of the low-cut dress was also so wide and loose that every moment and with the slightest gesture, the nipple of one or the other breast would escape the bodice, followed by the entire breast. Absently, without stopping talking or laughing, Malini would then cup her naked breast in her palm, squeezing its rounded curves gently, feeling its weight, and would tickle with one finger its nipple, which was small, hard and pointed, and surrounded by a tiny sparkling pearled ruff. Then the young girl – or rather, young wife – still quite absent-mindedly, it seemed, would replace the breast under the thin material. The other breast would at once pop out.

I've already mentioned that the gown Malini wore on this occasion and which she had even worn to church, was of see-through material almost as clear as ordinary window-glass. One could therefore constantly observe the pleasing shape and curly golden texture of that thatch the pubic bone set into relief, which also emphasized the firm-muscled line of a gymnast's stomach and long slim thighs. More than any other aspect of her beauty I think this convinced me that I had to possess this woman sexually, to have her properly there and then, on the spot.

To be absolutely precise this decision was taken at the very moment when Malini sat down and invited the priest and myself to sit opposite her and sample some more cakes. With the same movement she pulled up her skirt with both hands, half-apologetically as if she realized the diaphanous screen of material between her body and ourselves was positively indecent. She lifted the mass of muslin to the very tops of her legs, as far as her sex, so that we could see quite clearly the bright pink swell of the lips of her vulva and the open vertical slit between, dark and (I imagined) humid below the blonde triangle.

The lower apex of the latter ended with the same clarity of definition, without excess hairs or fringe at the very spot where one saw, or thought one saw, the clitoris pulse like the heart of a dawning star.

Malini watched us looking at her sex. She seemed to be waiting, but for what? For us to compliment her on her splendid display? The priest shook his head once again.

Just to make sure I wasn't seeing things, I asked my witness:

'Have you ever seen anything so lovely?'

'Never!' he said.

Then I said to her:

'Why has Andreas waited so long without making love to you?' She smiled happily.

'Without making love to me? Whatever makes you think that?'

'You can make love without losing your virginity,' her mother explained to me.

'Why limit yourself?' I wanted to know. I took the priest to task: 'Is that the result of your teaching?'

He shrugged.

'Anyway, what do *you* know about sex?' Malini challenged me. 'Fucking is limited too.'

'Does Andreas bugger you?' I asked her.

The way she pursed her lips seemed to mimic the look of her sex. She ended up admitting:

'Not yet. He likes to go by stages.'

'What about you? What'll be your next step?'

She remained motionless, silent, inscrutable. I wanted to be the next step and I told her so, adding:

'You are so feminine that it makes me want to take you like a boy.'

Her laugh rang out again. She got up and touched my elbow with her right hand.

'Let's go and find Andreas again,' she said. 'We've been married over an hour and we haven't even spoke to each other!'

She and I chatted with her husband, amused the guests, danced, drank, ate and were merry till nightfall. Then I took her hand and led her into her room.

'On the marriage bed?' she teased.

But she didn't wait for me to make a move. Standing where she was she raised her skirt in the way that only she knew how. This time she didn't stop at groin level: she pulled it right over her head, flung it at arm's length right across the room and stood before me, infinitely beautiful, young and naked.

I completed the loss of her virginity. Then I penetrated her anally. Then orally. Then again into the gash whose pert expression seemed to go on questioning me, and from which ran a thin trickle of blood.

'Now what am I?' she said. 'Girl or boy or both?'

She didn't let me answer that, though.

'That depends on Andreas,' she declared. 'It's what he wants that matters more than anything to me.'

During the year that followed I never was quite sure whether she had told her husband about our relationship. As for myself, I made no secret of my feelings for her. I used to see her every day and would treat her intimately and tenderly in front of her husband. But in order to make love she and I would go round to her mother's or to the priest's house.

On their wedding anniversay Andreas and she invited me to accompany them to a nightclub. None of us had been there before and so we weren't members. At the very moment when we were ingenuously trying to talk our way in, a young man with an angelic expression came out: he was a complete stranger but he swore blind he was a friend of ours and would vouch for us. Then, along with his sponsorship, he offered us a full bottle of whisky, disappearing without our even catching his name.

We'd come to dance, but the shiny metallic expanse that served as the dance-floor was too crowded. We ogled other people and their reflections in the mirrors, and drank our friend's whisky.

Usually in places of this sort you can't see or hear. The strobe lighting alternates with the ritual darkness and is meant to blind you, while the music is amplified to effectively deafen you. But this place was rather different: the lights and sounds were soft and the atmosphere as a result was relaxed and easygoing. The young men dancing with their girls didn't look aggressive and the girls were on the whole attractive, although the fashion in clothes at the time wasn't flattering to most of them.

Andreas declared that despite all the follies and disasters from which mankind had suffered, the absurdity of clothes – their ever-increasing ugliness and mythical role – was one of the more alarming phenomena. Instead of dressing to make themselves more attractive, human beings turned themselves into dressed-up monkeys. Clothes had become a cause, rather than a consequence, of their bigotry, peevishness and stupidity. Dressed in such a frigid fashion, how could they love?

'The magnitude of the catastrophe came home to me clearly one afternoon on the terrace of the Café Florian on the Piazza San Marco in Venice,' he continued. 'Like Jehovah promising an amnesty for Sodom and Gomorrah, I told myself that if I saw just one man or woman wearing an outfit which didn't actually nauseate me, I would forgive the human race. I lost my bargain.'

'Maybe those holidaymakers were such an awful sight only because they were *half* dressed?' I suggested.

'Quite,' he agreed. 'One must never do things by halves.'

'How am I at the moment?' wondered Malini, 'am I dressed enough or not naked enough?'

'When you were half-virginal,' replied Andreas, 'did you feel too much of a woman or not loved enough?'

Malini rose and beckoned to the nearest waiter. When he reached her she took off her dress and handed it to him. The man bowed and took it away, to the cloakroom, no doubt. Malini sat down again with a contented smile.

'Andreas is right,' she said. 'I was half at ease. Now I'm absolutely comfortable.'

We went on talking without worrying about the people there. Anyhow, no one seemed shocked by Malini's nakedness. The looks she received were only of admiration and respect.

Quite naturally Andreas and I ended up kissing and caressing her. She reciprocated and would have made love with us there and then in front of everyone, had we ourselves dared do so. But we were still only half free and consequently half brave.

'I love you,' Malini said to Andreas. 'Why do I need a lover as well?'

We had finished the bottle. Andreas used drunkenness as a pretext for sincerity:

'Every couple has the sense of there being a missing half. Only another man can fill that void a man opens up in a woman. Getting married means going into partnership together to find that other man. Love is solitude until it achieves impossible inclusions.'

When we left the porter ceremoniously held out Malini's dress for her. She shook her head and laughed.

'No thanks,' she explained. 'I'm not cold any more.'

That night I made love to Malini for the first time in the presence of her husband. And they made love in front of me.

'But why not all three together?' she said, surprised. 'In the arms of just one man I feel half-neglected. Half a virgin. Half naked. Half alone. Half loved.'

'So that we can love you the way you want,' I said, putting my thoughts into words, 'Andreas will have to learn to make love with me too.'

'Haven't I done just that already?' he remonstrated. 'When I talk to you and we spent hours and days together talking about Nature and books, dreaming about friendship, hating injustice, desiring life, waiting for death – aren't we making love?'

I thought about that: tomorrow I'll tell Andreas that he's wrong to suggest that I should be his child's only physical father. Would it be rational for this human-to-be to have only half a father? Would it be fair if it were only half-created?

Two bodies can reproduce only one new weak body. Two hearts can form only one new sad heart. Two brains can remake only one limited brain. In order for our child to escape this tragic genetic inevitability, Andreas's body must unite with mine inside Malini's body: there his heart already awaits me, there, where our thoughts already meet.

When, inside our beloved wife, our naked lover, nothing distinguishes Andreas from myself any longer nor separates us from her; when Malini no longer chooses between lover and husband; when I see no difference between her and Andreas; when Andreas no longer knows whether he's making love to Malini or myself; when our sexes and rights are finally indistinguishable and we no longer split our ideas, ourselves, and our possessions into half – perhaps the three of us will be happy enough, inventive enough and potent enough to perpetuate ourselves in the genes of a child as yet unborn.

VI. Coda to the Siren's Song

Derailment at Honfleur

I don't need to go where I am going: I'm already there.

Ton-Hon

'At Honfleur Emmanuelle boards the train which is to take her to Lisieux. She immediately likes the smell of this station, which reminds her of her childhood . . .'

Thus begins a parody recently published by André Balland, under the title *Emmanuelle in the railcar*, emanating from the bestselling pens of two former participants in the events of May 1968 who have now become mere jokers in their old age, Michel-Antoine Burnier and Patrick Rambaud.

Everything is possible: Emmanuelle might even leave this earth altogether, but what a bloody silly idea to go and leave from Honfleur!

Love of the sea doesn't explain it all. Regular visitors to the Normandy port will at once have understood that the subconscious reason for this choice is to be found in the architecture of the Lieutenancy.

Like so many ancient things, this ex-residence of the royal lieutenant-governors overlooking the Old Docks, no longer has any special function. Taking a closer look at it, one even doubts whether it could ever have served its turn for what it was. Its doorway, apparently borrowed from the ramparts of Caen, leads nowhere. The staircase up its façade opens on to empty space. Its windows look out upon useless walls. It's a building one may skirt but would never think of entering: what'd one do inside?

What connection is there between this run-of-the-mill edifice and the unclassifiable Emmanuelle? None, except for the following moral parallels.

From a rather relativistic view of the Lieutenancy, Nitya Phenkun in *Last words of the Kinnari*, draws a series of conclusions which at first glance all seem incontestible:

(1) What is made any old how is worth nothing!

(2) Doing no matter what is worse than doing nothing.

(3) Going no matter where is going nowhere.

The theory becomes more complicated the moment the author realizes that the architectural interest (let's say, to obscure the matter even more, the cultural worth) of the Lieutenancy is not substantially affected by the absurdities of its construction. Without withdrawing the earlier propositions, Nitya Phenkun suggests three further ones, diametrically opposed to the former and no less pertinent, namely:

(1) What is made any old how is always something.

(2) Doing no matter what is better than doing nothing.

(3) Going no matter where is going somewhere.

Bearing in mind the simultaneous validity of these contrary hypotheses one shouldn't be surprised that they lead to the formulation of two *Honfleur Principles*, proven and yet opposed, whose prime function consists of causing us similar despair.

The first of these states that *Those who have no blueprint for life are inevitably disappointed*.

Which leads one back to supposing that certain people do have plans for their lives? Anyway, let's hop on to the train steps before it pulls out of this station which awakens such nice memories in Emmanuelle, and let's shout loud enough for the departing traveller to hear our questions:

'Where are you going? What will you do? How will you do it?'

Her answer, predictably, is drowned by the train whistle. Luckily she has enough time to throw us a packet wrapped in pale blue material and embroidered in pink. Love letters? No – her school textbooks.

On the cover of the first, under the pupil's name and her age (fourteen) we read the already adult handwriting: *I'll make my life a dream and make the dream a reality.*

Here apparently is confirmation of the first Principle of Honfleur. Emmanuelle has had a meaningful, full, peaceful, happy life – the opposite of that contingent existence whose very idea gave us the creeps in our own youth – because she hasn't just rushed blindly onward. At least she has chosen the places she's wanted to live in, if not her country of origin. She has chosen her language, her name, and her beliefs. She has chosen her friends and companions in life. She has chosen her work and her pleasures, her solitude and rebellion too. She has taken risks and had ideas. And since she hasn't told us that she has any regrets about her choices, it must mean that she regrets nothing.

All well and good, so let's move on to the Second Principle. What does that teach us?

Those who live according to plan are inevitably disappointed.

Yes, but whoever would dispute that? Everyone knows quite well that no hope is ever realized. What reality can ever satisfy someone who drugs himself with ideal inventions? What present can interest him, if he only dreams of the future? How much time is left him to enjoy, when he only knows how to desire? What restriction can he stand when freedom awaits him behind his own closed eyelids? He won't agree to anything, anywhere, anyhow, because he doesn't want to act like a fool. So he plays the angel. Until the Fall.

Villiers de l'Isle Adam, whom I mentioned elsewhere,

dreamed up a 'future Eve' more perfect than any creature of God or the Devil ever was or will be. Indeed, to be quite sure that she wouldn't be botched, the author took care to have her made here on earth and by the hand of man. A fine plan! Just about every other man or woman has had the same idea. The result: on the eve of his death the poet, worn out by the dog's life he'd had, cried out with sardonic humour 'Ah, I shan't forget this planet!'

To sum up all this, Nitya's six propositions are equally horrible – all true and all deadly. And heads or tails their principles enunciate the same destiny: human life is doomed to pure deception even more inexorably than to death.

To dream of living, dream her life, act out her dream . . . Emmanuelle is by no means alone in believing such a scheme possible. She and those like her would perhaps have done better to ask themselves first of all whether life is a promise which can be kept.

Not to keep one's promise is the sign of dishonesty. Apposite question: is life fair to us? Whence does our failure spring? And why in the first place do other people deceive us so? . . . Ah, now things don't look too bright!

But for god's sake, there must be somebody somewhere who dies quite happy for having lived at all? Yet if we were to meet one of these rare birds, how could we trust what they said? Maybe they'd be prematurely senile? Without realizing he already had one foot in the grave, such a person would play the role of adman (on the strength of which he had drawn a small loan) for just one minute more than required. Witness Georges Bataille jabbering 'I don't want to boast, but death seems to me the most ludicrous thing in the world.' Witness Jorge Luis Borges, no less euphoric and sanctimonious, simpering to the young girl interviewing him: 'Life is fine but one mustn't misuse it.' But what are you talking about here, doctor? Misusing life? What does that mean, in plain terms? How can one misuse something of which one has such a stingy ration? How can one misuse a piece of luck one scarcely has time to glimpse, let alone understand, and which is beyond your grasp before you've begun to understand what it might mean? You're trying to take us for a ride, Mr Writer!

Jean Paulhan was more honest than these demystifiers of Thanatos, and represented the discreet ambition of the human race in general when, asked about death, he replied: 'I hope to live till mine.' Isn't this masterpiece of *scaramanzia* worth more than just another confession of ignorance, a shrug of the shoulders or any scream of fear? Is the awful modesty of this wish the surest way of invoking the final lucidity lying in wait: *I've lived only according to plan, so I haven't lived at all?* No: there's no counter-proposition to the Honfleur Principles. No third postulate. The children of the night shall remain in darkness.

So fuck the lot of them! Train, Lieutenancy and all! But not before we first install, along with our charges of dynamite, a microphone which will pick up Emmanuelle's last words.

But the girl will surprise to the very end! She doesn't emit the satisfied gurgle her fans are expecting of her, something in this style: 'I've desired everything, wanted to know everything, have tried everything, and dared all. I've loved fully and had a ball. I die happy.' Nor does she paraphrase the epitaph of James Bond as Ian Fleming, himself near death, is supposed to have worded it: 'I didn't waste time by trying to spin it out. I've lived out my time.' Instead of that final affirmation of her dreams, which we've been waiting for for so long, Emmanuelle gives us a farewell speech which leaves us somewhat baffled – a rather long farewell, obviously, since even her last breath doesn't succeed in being concise:

'I feel solidarity with the sufferings of others, of those who live without cause for hope. It is right for them to want to commit suicide. It would not be right for me to survive them.'